ChangelingPress.com

Rooster/Cuffs & Kink Duet

Harley Wylde

Rooster/Cuffs & Kink Duet
Harley Wylde

ISBN: 978-1-60521-814-4

Publisher:
Changeling Press LLC
315 N. Centre St.
Martinsburg, WV 25404
ChangelingPress.com

Printed in the U.S.A.

Editor: Crystal Esau
Cover Artist: Bryan Keller

The individual stories in this anthology have been previously released in E-Book format.

Table of Contents

Rooster (Devil's Boneyard MC 8)
Harley Wylde

Alora -- I've prided myself on being a strong, independent woman and not needing anyone. I didn't become a bestselling author by the age of twenty out of pure dumb luck. I worked my tail off to get as far as I have. But there are few perks to having a man in my life. Laughter, romance, and companionship. Battery operated boyfriends can only do so much. Too bad the guy who sets me on fire is a bossy biker who wants to claim me. No way I'm letting him label me as property. Nope. Not happening. Doesn't matter if he does make my knees weak and my heart race. I'm not giving in!

Rooster -- Of all the women to capture my interest, it had to be the most stubborn, sexy, adorable woman on the planet. I love her mind, her sense of humor, and the way she fills out a pair of shorts. I don't even mind that she's an exhibitionist, as long as no one touches. Doesn't matter to me her uncles were both rotten to the core. The Devil's Fury may think she belongs to them, but I have other plans. Alora will be mine -- no matter the cost.

Chapter One
"A dirty mind is a terrible thing to waste."
-- Ouiser Boudreaux

Alora

I nearly danced my way to the mailbox, eager to see if my package had arrived. I yanked open the metal door and squealed when I saw the box inside. Pulling it out, I turned it over in my hands, noticing there was a return address with no company name. Anticipation hummed in my veins. The contents of this unsuspecting box would break my writer's block and I'd finally be able to finish my novel. Preferably before my editor came after me with a pitchfork... or worse. I grabbed the other mail and shoved the mailbox shut before hurrying up the walkway.

I rushed into the house, letting the door slam behind me. The rest of the mail fell to the floor as I ripped into the package. While I'd been eager to try everything inside, the wireless egg held my attention. I couldn't remember the last time I'd had a satisfactory orgasm. It had caused a dry spell in my writing. How could I write about sex when I hadn't experienced the euphoria of a release in months? Not to mention my character reviewed sex toys for her blog. Not knowing how they worked made it difficult to write a believable scene.

Gypsy, my Akita, circled my feet. The spoiled diva knew her toys arrived by mail in a box similar to the one in my hands and probably thought I had something for her. I stared her down, holding my treasure up higher. "Not for you! These are Mommy's toys."

She whined and pawed at my leg, eyeing the

cardboard box. I knew she'd never leave me in peace if I didn't give her something. I took a quick detour to the kitchen and grabbed an antler from the mixed pack of chews I'd picked up at the store for her. I tossed it and Gypsy snatched it mid-air, running off with her tail wagging.

"You're welcome!" I yelled after her. I'd only had the rotten puppy for two months, but she'd already gotten huge. I had to admit she was super smart. She'd been house trained within two weeks.

Carrying the box up the stairs to my bedroom, I dropped it onto the mattress and squirmed in place as I ripped into the individual packages. A vibrating anal plug, another vibrator with dual penetration and clit stimulation, some vibrating nipple clamps, a rabbit with guaranteed G-spot stimulation, and the holy grail -- my wireless egg! All but the last two ran on regular batteries so I carried my two precious items over to the dresser. Since these were just the latest in a long line of products I'd tried before using them in a book, I kept a power bank on the corner of my dresser.

I plugged in both toys before retrieving batteries for the others. I'd made sure everything was waterproof because who didn't love having a bit of fun in the shower or tub? Once the other toys were ready to go, I placed them on the bathroom counter and decided to set the scene.

I'd left my character in the bath, alone and moping. While the tub filled with steamy water, I went downstairs to pour myself a glass of wine. Checking on Gypsy first, I smiled when I saw her sprawled across her bed, gnawing on the antler. She'd stay busy for a while.

When I got back to the bathroom, I set the wine on the ledge of the tub and pulled out a thick, fluffy towel. I stripped out of my clothes, set the toys within reach, and climbed into the heavenly water. Sighing, I closed my eyes and leaned back. I'd tried this very thing multiple times already. Without success of breaking through and figuring out my book. I blamed a lack of sex. Which explained the toys just waiting for me to give them a try.

I also blamed one hot, sexy biker who'd ruined me for other men. Ever since my short fling with Colorado, I hadn't found a single man who piqued my interest. But Colorado had made it clear he wasn't ready to settle down. Or rather, he didn't want a relationship with *me*. I hadn't taken it to heart and had enjoyed our few days together. Even if I'd been at the Devil's Fury compound for less-than-ideal reasons, at least I'd gotten something out of it.

And a cousin. I'd gotten my cousin, Meredith, out of the deal too. I'd had no idea my uncle had been part of the Devil's Fury, or that he'd had a daughter. From what I'd learned about him while I was there, and my other uncle, Saul, I could see why my mother insisted she was an only child. But Meredith was great, and I'd had a blast getting to know her!

I shook the thoughts from my head, not wanting to think too much about Colorado or the Devil's Fury. After the incident, I'd moved to another town. Since I wrote for a living, it didn't matter where I called home. As long as I had wi-fi and electricity, nothing else mattered. So I'd picked up and moved to Florida.

If the eye candy I saw around town, wearing cuts that said *Devil's Boneyard*, would give me the time of day, I wouldn't be in this predicament. I hadn't told anyone I was related to the Devil's Fury and didn't plan to. But I had to wonder if I'd have a better shot at one of the yummy bikers if I did admit to my ties to another club. Unless they were rivals. I shivered. Yeah, not going to take the chance.

I took a sip of my wine and leaned back in the tub, closing my eyes a moment. I breathed in and out, deep breaths meant to calm me. My mind had a tendency to wander, which kept me tense all the damn time. I took another swallow of my wine and cupped my breast. The alcohol coated my tongue as I pinched and tugged at my nipple. I rolled the tip until it plumped up. I set the glass aside and reached for the nipple clamps. I clipped one to the hard peak I'd been toying with and turned it on.

"Oh! Now that's nice." I bit my lip as I adjusted the vibration, turning it up a little. I played with the other side until I could attach the second clamp. "Oh yeah."

My hips shifted as my clit started to pulse with need. So far, I was loving my latest purchases. I only hoped it had the desired effect. Well, two. I wanted to come so hard I'd exorcise the demons so to speak, and I needed to finish my damn book. If this didn't give me a breakthrough, my writing career would be over. I had a week to get my book to my editor. One. Week. And how far had I gotten? Chapter three… of twenty-eight. I had a feeling I'd be throwing out the plot I'd written before I'd started the book. I didn't know why I bothered trying. It never worked.

The doorbell rang downstairs making me growl in frustration. I wasn't getting up to answer it! Absolutely not! It rang three more times before whoever had stopped by decided to give up. I sighed and tried to get back in the mood. I swirled my fingers over my clit and eyed the other toys I'd brought into the bathroom with me. I picked up the dual-penetration vibrator and turned it on. It hummed as I lowered it beneath the water. I used one of the rounded tips to tease my clit some more before sliding the toy down further.

It took a little teasing and finessing, but I finally got it into position. The smooth end in my ass pressed against the longer, thicker part in my pussy. I turned it up another notch and gasped as the top nub worked my clit. All it took was a slight rocking of my hips and it felt like every nerve in my body was lighting up. I came so fast and hard I nearly blacked out, my throat sore from screaming out in pleasure.

I heard a crash downstairs, lots of barking, and heavy steps pounding up the stairs. I tried to shake the stars from my eyes, but the toy kept buzzing and soon I was coming again. My back arched, my ass pressing down harder on the toy, and the scream that tore through me made my throat hurt even more. The bathroom door crashed open, and I blinked at a police officer.

"Um." He stared at me, mouth open, before slowly straightening and stepping back. "I thought someone was hurt."

I'd forgotten to turn off the toys and felt another orgasm building. I whimpered and reached for them. I managed to shut off the nipple clamps and tossed them aside, but the other toy kept going and before I could remove it, I was coming again.

Sweet baby Jesus! I wasn't sure if I wanted it to stop or invite the hot cop to join me. And yeah, I'd noticed his broad chest, bulging biceps, and the long, thick cock that was getting harder by the moment. I moaned and shut my eyes, wondering if it would be possible for the earth to open up and swallow me whole.

I reached down and removed the toy, shutting it

off. I panted for breath, my eyes opening just enough to see the officer still gaping at me. Not the way I wanted to introduce myself to the local law. *Shit.*

"Ma'am, um... There's an IRS auditor downstairs who wants to speak with you." His gaze skimmed over me, making my cheeks heat.

"I'm behind you," a man's voice said from inside my bedroom. "Ms. Danvers, I need to discuss your previous tax returns with you. You can't claim sex toys as a business cost."

I tipped my head back and laughed softly. "I will be happy to explain why they're a tax write-off. Could you wait downstairs?"

The officer was still staring at me and I watched him. He was young, but probably older than me. Cute. And definitely checking me out. He cleared his throat and reached down to adjust himself. I should have been embarrassed, or screaming my head off at having a strange man in the bathroom while I lay naked in the tub. At least, a normal person would have probably reacted that way. Good thing I'd never claimed to be normal.

"Officer, if you're going to stand there and stare, could you at least help me out of the tub? I'm not sure my legs still work. I don't think I've ever come that hard before. Definitely leaving a review on that one!"

He seemed to snap out of it, his cheeks flushing, as he stumbled forward and held out his hand. I grasped it and let him haul me to my feet. The water cascaded down my body as I reached for the towel, accidentally knocking the toys to the floor. He picked up the dual-penetration vibrator, eyed the three rounded tips before his gaze slid over me again.

I took it from him and decided to explain, since he was clearly curious. His girlfriend or future wife would thank me later.

"This one," I said point to the shorter tip, "buzzes against my clit. The middle one goes inside my pussy, and the third goes in my ass."

He audibly gulped, the heat in his eyes nearly searing me as he looked me over again. As tempted as I was to ask if he'd like a demonstration, I refrained. Barely. But the shock factor might have been worth it.

I wrapped the towel around me and went into the bedroom where I pulled out a tank and set of pajama shorts. I slipped them on, forgoing a bra and panties, then led the way downstairs to the living room, where I found the IRS auditor pacing. He wasn't much taller than me, a bit soft around the middle, and his glasses kept sliding down his nose. Not bad if you were into the geeky type. The officer behind me was more my speed though.

"What can I do for you?" I asked the auditor.

"I need to see your receipts and your tax forms for the last two years. And then we need to discuss what is and isn't a business expense," he said, staring at me down his nose.

Pompous ass!

"First off, I'll gladly get those items for you. They're in my office. Secondly, the sex toys *are* a business expense, and if you'd read any of my books, you'd know that. Each and every toy has featured in my books. If I don't know firsthand how they work, I can't write a believable scene with them. I'd offer a demonstration, but it would probably give you heart failure."

The officer behind me muttered something that sounded like *I want one.*

The IRS auditor gaped at me and I resisted the urge to reach over and close his mouth. While he processed my words, I went to my office and retrieved my tax files and receipts, as well as the flash drive where I'd scanned everything and kept a digital copy. The officer followed me through the house, and I glanced at him over my shoulder.

"Why exactly are you here?" I asked.

"The auditor has had some trouble before, of the violent kind, so I was sent along to make sure you didn't get out of hand." He eyed me. "You definitely aren't the sort I typically would protect him from. Not that I'm complaining."

"I bet you say that to all the women you catch masturbating in their tubs," I said.

"You're very calm about all this."

I shrugged a shoulder. "Not the first time someone has seen me naked. I was a stripper for a few months. While I hadn't exactly been shy to begin with, after taking off my clothes for money, it desensitized me to people seeing me naked. Not to mention, I rather liked having an audience."

He cleared his throat and gazed straight ahead. "If I may say so, I'd gladly be your audience any day."

I paused and placed a hand on my hip. "Why, Officer, are you flirting with me?"

"If you can't tell, I must be doing it wrong." He winked. "And the name is Officer Tim Murray. But you can call me anything you want, as long as you call me."

I snorted and rolled my eyes, continuing down the hall back to the auditor. "Does that line ever actually work for you?"

"Sometimes. Is it working now?"

"Not even a little." I smirked and entered the living room, handing the files and flash drive to the auditor. He leafed through the documents before taking a seat. I noticed he had a laptop bag strapped across him. I hoped like hell this wasn't going to take long. The bliss from my orgasm had faded and now I was just getting annoyed.

The front door nearly rattled off the hinges when someone started pounding on it. If I hadn't known King Kong was a fictional character, I'd think he was on my porch. What the hell?

I narrowed my eyes in the direction of the front entry and went to answer it. It wasn't like I knew anyone in town. I'd only been here a month, which made it doubtful I'd pissed anyone off -- yet. I yanked it open, ready to tear into whoever was on the other side, but stopped and stared.

The man arched his eyebrows and tipped his sunglasses down enough to peer over the top of them. God, why did I find that so sexy? He'd braced an arm against the doorframe and his muscles bulged. I licked my lips and tried to remember how to speak. As my gaze skimmed over him, it snagged on the black leather over his shoulders. *Fuck.* It was one of the bikers.

Rooster -- Devil's Boneyard MC.

"You going to let me in, *a ghrá*?"

His voice sent chills down my spine and my nipples hardened against my thin tank. He smirked, clearly knowing the effect he had on me. *Asshole.*

"I don't let strangers into my home," I said. I peered over his shoulder and saw another man on a motorcycle at the curb. It seemed only one of them wanted to come into the house. Thank goodness for small favors.

He leaned in, the scent of cinnamon and cloves making me want to breathe in deep. "But we're not strangers. You're Twister's niece, which makes you

Devil's Fury property. Since we consider them family, that makes you mine."

My knees nearly buckled at his words. *His*? I wasn't sure I'd survive belonging to someone like him. He made Colorado seem more like a puppy. And that Irish lilt to his words! Holy hell. If I'd been wearing panties, they'd have been soaked. As it was, my pajamas shorts were getting an embarrassing wet spot on them. I hoped like hell no one noticed.

I felt the heat of someone behind me. The growl from the biker told me it was probably Officer Murray. Why did I get the feeling everything was about to go to shit? So much for multiple orgasms and writing three chapters before midnight. I sighed and stepped back, elbowing the officer out of the way so Rooster could step into the house.

Gypsy, traitor that she was, immediately went to Rooster and rubbed against him, begging for attention. *Same, girl. Same.* As he scratched behind her ears, I wondered what those hands would feel like on my body.

"Want me to take out the trash?" Rooster asked, eyeing Officer Murray.

"He's here with the IRS auditor," I said.

Rooster folded his arms. "You're being audited? What the fuck for?"

My cheeks warmed. "Um…"

"She claimed sex toys on her return," the auditor yelled out from the other room.

Were we just telling everyone that shit now? Wasn't there a confidentiality clause or something? Rooster covered his mouth, but it didn't do any good. I'd seen the smile and heard the snicker he'd let slip loose. Damnit. Now he'd go back to his biker brothers and word would spread. The romance author was buying sex toys and writing them off on her taxes. I could just imagine the types of calls and invitations I'd receive after that news hit the clubhouse. Fuck my life.

"Why are you here?" I asked, tipping my chin up to hold his gaze.

He glanced over at the officer. "Heard there was trouble at your place. I was in the area."

"Wait." I held up a hand. "You heard? What does that mean? Do you have people spying on me?"

He scratched the short beard along his jaw. "Not exactly spying. More like keeping watch for unsavory types. When Badger asks for a favor, which is rare in case you were wondering, we tend to do as he asks. He was worried when you up and moved with no word."

I shook my head, trying to make sense of it all. One, how the hell had they known where I'd moved to? And two, why the hell did it matter? So what if my uncle had been part of their club? My mother hadn't had anything to do with her brothers, and I wasn't sure I wanted anything to do with the Devil's Fury either. My fling with Colorado had been fun. He hadn't wanted to keep me long-term, and honestly, I didn't think I was ready for that sort of thing.

"How did you know she was here?" Officer Murray asked. "I get the feeling she didn't share the information with anyone."

Rooster grinned. "GPS."

Mother. Fucker. They'd hacked my damn phone? Or maybe it was my car. Since I had that On-Star thing they could probably find my car anywhere in the world. Damnit. I pinched the bridge of my nose and wondered how the hell I ended up in this predicament. Alpha men were sexy in books, and in theory, but in real life? I wasn't sure I was equipped to handle one, much less two clubs of them.

"I need a drink," I muttered and left the idiots in the front entry while I went to get the wine from the fridge. Too bad I didn't have anything stronger.

Chapter Two

"Sex is a two-way treat."
        -- Franklin P. Jones

Rooster

I hadn't lied. Not entirely.

Badger had let us know when Alora disappeared and the For Sale sign went up at her house. Outlaw had been able to use the GPS in her phone and car to track her to our town. After getting a picture of her, it hadn't been hard to keep an eye out. She'd shown her face in town within a few days of the call and one of my brothers had followed her back to this neighborhood and gotten her address. Since then, I'd been keeping watch over her.

Charming had ordered me to watch over her. I'd been ticked at first, not caring much for babysitting duty. Then I'd seen her, and I'd done it because I wanted to. Admittedly, I might have taken things a little too far. I'd made sure a few neighbors discreetly observed her and let me know if anything suspicious seemed to be going on. Like an officer breaking into her house while she screamed her damn head off. I wanted to know what the screaming had been about, but I wasn't going to ask while fuck face and the auditor were here.

I watched her ass sway as she made her way to the kitchen. The fact the asshole cop was watching too made me want to punch him. Fucker had no right to be eyeing her like some pervert. She was club property, whether she liked it or not. Since my brothers knew I'd called dibs on her, none of them would lay a hand on her. Not even if she flirted with every single one.

I'd heard about her time with Colorado. I'd

wondered why he'd let her leave, but after a quick call, he'd assured me he didn't have a claim on her. It seemed they'd only been having fun. Blind fucker! Or more like stupid. Either way, she might be Devil's Fury by blood, but soon enough she'd be mine. I'd already started my research because I needed to know what made her tick.

It hadn't taken much digging to discover she wrote books for a living. I'd figured a good way to get to know her was to see what types of things she wrote about. I'd searched for everything she had available. I'd read each and every one. Granted, I'd downloaded them to my phone so my brothers wouldn't give me shit about reading romances, but holy hell! If the woman had done any of the things she'd written about, I knew she'd be wild in the bedroom. I only hoped she gave me a chance to find out. Not that women typically told me no.

Except Farrah. I'd had a crush on Venom's oldest daughter, until she'd ended up with Demon. It had been clear pretty quick those two belonged together. Farrah had been a firebrand, and I'd looked forward to taming her, but it wasn't meant to be. I hadn't been in love with her, so I'd backed off and let Demon wrangle her.

"I think Miss Danvers has made it clear she doesn't want you here," Officer Murray said.

"Really? I could have sworn all the eye fucking meant I was welcome to stay." I smirked when he scowled at me. Yeah, I knew the shithead wanted in her pants. Wasn't happening on my watch. I knew all about Tim Murray, and every other cop in town. While he wasn't on the take, he wasn't exactly angelic either. Word on the street was that he let women out of traffic violations if they gave him a little something in return.

If he even tried to pull that shit with Alora, I'd make his life a living hell.

She came back from the kitchen, a glass clutched in her hand, so full it nearly overflowed. I bit the inside of my cheek so I wouldn't smile. It was the biggest fucking glass I'd ever seen, and I wondered if she'd poured the entire bottle into the damn thing. She took a gulp and went into the living room. I followed, leaning against the doorframe as she made herself comfortable on the couch, clearly not caring that she was barely dressed in front of three men. I might have gotten pissed about it if I didn't find it so entertaining to watch them squirm.

The auditor used a handkerchief to wipe his brow, but I noticed the bulge in his pants and the way he tried to hunch over to hide it from her. His cheeks were flushed a deep pink and his hands trembled as he went through her files. As much as I didn't like these two getting an eyeful of her, it was amusing as hell to see the auditor so flustered. I had to wonder when the last time was he saw this much skin on a woman without paying for the pleasure. Even the cop beside me was doing his best to hide his reaction to her.

I cleared my throat to get Alora's attention. She narrowed her eyes at me. If she thought it would scare me off, she was dead wrong. I liked her spitting and hissing like a little kitten. Made me wonder what it would take to get her to purr.

"Baby girl, you might want to uh…" I gestured to her clothes. The strap of her tank had fallen off and she was dangerously close to exposing her breast to everyone.

She snorted and rolled her eyes, but I noticed she tugged it back into place. "Wouldn't matter. They already got an eyeful."

I straightened. "What the fuck does that mean?"

"It means I was naked when Officer Murray over there decided to break into my house. They caught me in the tub, bare as the day I was born."

"Door was unlocked," the dickhead said. "And you were screaming. I thought you might be injured or in trouble."

Now things were getting interesting. No fucking way the door was unlocked. I'd noticed the busted latch. Even though it still shut, it had clearly been forced open. I'd make sure it was taken care of before the night was over. I pushed off the doorframe and approached Alora. I leaned down, bracing a hand on either side of her, and placed my lips near her ear. "Screaming in the tub, hm? I might need a demonstration of what exactly you were doing at the time."

I heard her breath catch and smiled as I pulled back. Her cheeks had flushed a pretty pink and I noticed her nipples had pebbled against her shirt. I couldn't wait for the two jokers to leave so I could see if the little kitten wanted to play. Fuck but she was sexy as hell!

The auditor cleared his throat. "Miss Danvers, these are the receipts the IRS has deemed inappropriate for a tax write-off."

She reached over and snatched the papers from him. I skimmed over them and nearly choked when I realized exactly why the IRS had sent someone to her house. Fuck me! The woman had written off sex toys? And not just a few. There had to be at least fifteen on that list.

"I already explained why I wrote them off," Alora said, putting the receipts down. "I needed to study them to find out how they worked so I could use them in my books. My character has a blog where she reviews these products. I couldn't very well explain how they worked or felt if I hadn't used them myself. I mean, I guess I could have, but it wouldn't have been accurate."

The two argued back and forth and I'd decided I had enough. I called the club's lawyer. Celeste answered on the second ring, and by the breathless sound of her voice, I'd either interrupted a heated argument or something more fun.

"What do you want, Rooster?" she demanded.

"Need your help. My girl is getting audited by the IRS. I'll text you the address."

She huffed. "Fine. I'm on my way, but you owe me."

I smirked. So I hadn't interrupted an argument. I disconnected the call and texted Alora's full name and address to her. The little writer was getting all worked up, and if she weren't clutching her wine like it was a precious gem, I figured she'd have tossed it at the auditor already. The guy was a pompous ass, and clearly hadn't been laid in a long ass time. If ever.

Ten minutes later, I heard the front door open and shut and saw Celeste striding into the house. She had sex hair that she'd attempted to smooth out, but it hadn't done much good. Especially since her blouse had been mis-buttoned. I wasn't about to bring it to her attention. Woman would probably cut off my balls, and I was rather attached to them.

"You don't knock anymore?" I asked.

She rolled her eyes and discreetly flipped me off. I covered my mouth to hide my smile. Yeah, she still had fire to her.

"What is the meaning of this?" Celeste demanded.

"Who are you?" Officer Murray asked.

"Celeste Dubois, Attorney at Law. I'm here to represent the interests of Miss Danvers. Now explain to me why my client is being audited." Celeste sat next to Alora.

Bonus points to the cute writer for not asking who the hell Celeste was or why she was here. She'd either heard my conversation, even in the midst of her argument, or she was good at just rolling with whatever life threw her way.

The auditor showed Celeste the receipts and explained Alora had written them off as business expenses.

Celeste pulled out her reading glasses and skimmed the receipts, her lips twitching as she fought not to smile. "I see. And did my client explain *why* she'd written these off?"

Alora growled softly. "I've told him repeatedly I needed to know how those worked before I could use them in my books. Just looking them up online isn't always good enough, especially for this particular book series."

Celeste eyed the auditor over the rim of her glasses. "My client will need some time to gather the proof you need that these were legitimate expenses for her business. She'll pull the passages from her books where each item was used or mentioned. Since the list could be rather substantial, I'd like to request three days for Miss Danvers to get everything together."

"That's not how things are done." The auditor puffed up like he was about to go on a rant, but Celeste lifted a hand to stop him.

"Her books are published. It's not like she's going to fabricate evidence. I'll ensure that she writes down the page numbers that coincide with the published copies. We'll even provide you with the physical books so you can verify the accuracy of the information yourself." It sounded like she mumbled *it might do you some good*, but her professional exterior never once cracked. Except for the hair and blouse, but either no one else had noticed, or they didn't care. Now that I studied her, there was a gap where she'd skipped a buttonhole and Celeste was unknowingly flashing the auditor and cop every time she moved. The auditor's eyes seemed to glaze whenever he looked at Celeste, so he'd definitely noticed and had chosen not to tell her.

I knew the lawyer was a shark and she wouldn't hesitate to use every ploy she had, even if it meant letting strangers get a peek at her tits. Hell, once upon a time, she'd gotten paid for that very thing, since she'd covered the cost of her education by being a stripper. I knew for a fact, Celeste was proud of her body, and she'd flaunt it any chance she had. Much to Shade's dismay, since she was his baby cousin.

"I believe it's time for you gentlemen to leave," Alora said, standing and taking a gulp of her wine.

"Come on, boys. I'll walk you out," I said, gesturing toward the front door.

The auditor grumbled under his breath as he gathered his papers and shoved them into his satchel. Officer Murray had a glint in his eyes, and I knew he'd do his best to dig in his heels and stay. Not happening. I put myself between him and Alora and waited for him to take the hint. He snarled at me before turning on his heel and storming out of the house. The auditor trailed behind him like a puppy.

Once they'd cleared the front door, I shut it before returning to Alora and Celeste. Before I forgot, I shot off a text to one of the Prospects to come put a new lock on the door.

"I must say, Rooster, you do bring me some interesting cases," Celeste said.

"She's who you called?" Alora asked.

"When you were fighting with the auditor? Yeah. You looked like you were seconds from bashing him over the head with something. Although, if you were going to use one of the toys on that list to do it, I'd gladly invite him back in. As long as I got to watch."

She rolled her eyes at me and faced Celeste. "Is he always like this?"

"Rooster?" Celeste glanced at me before facing Alora again. "No. I think you bring out the best in him."

"If that's his best, I'm not sure I want to see his worst," Alora muttered.

"Oh, it's not my best," I assured her. "But if you'd like to bring that list of toys and head to your bedroom, I'd be happy to show you where I tend to excel. I still want to hear why you were screaming in the bathtub when they arrived."

Her face turned red as a tomato and her lips pressed together as she stared me down. Fuck but she was cute!

"And that's my cue to leave, but could I get one of your books first?" Celeste asked. "I'd love to read it tonight and get a better feel for how to best fight the IRS on this audit."

Alora gave her a smile. "You bet. In fact, I'll give you two and I'll sign them. Want a goody bag too?"

Celeste stood and tucked her hair behind her ear. "Goody bag?"

"Don't worry, I'll hook you up." Alora motioned for her to follow and I decided to see what she was up to. In her office, which was surprisingly neat and tidy,

Alora grabbed a small tote from the closet and two paperbacks. She signed them and tucked them into the bag before going over to a dresser that took up part of one wall. As she dug through the drawers, I saw her toss in a pen, what looked like lip balm, bookmarks, and other random book type items. When she threw in a handful of condoms, I couldn't help myself. I walked closer and reached into the drawer to pull one out.

"You have your name and book series printed on condoms?" I asked.

"Of course! They're fun to give away at book signings or conferences." Alora grabbed another handful and shoved them at me. "Take some. Maybe one of your conquests will end up checking out my books."

Celeste coughed to cover up a laugh. "Honey, you'd do better to toss those into the fishbowl at the clubhouse."

"Fishbowl?" Alora asked.

"There's a fishbowl behind the bar and it's stocked with condoms. Used to be where the club whores could get to it, until someone decided to poke holes in the condoms." Celeste smiled. "It was great meeting you. I'll read these and touch base with you tomorrow."

Celeste excused herself, leaving me alone with Alora… and a bunch of condoms. Oh the possibilities!

I eyed the wrappers in my hand before giving her the smile I'd been told dropped panties. Didn't work on my little ray of sunshine. Instead, she folded her arms over her chest and lifted her chin, staring me down.

"Don't even think about it," she said.

"Oh, I'm thinking all right. How about we *stop* thinking and get to the doing part?"

Chapter Three
"When I'm good, I'm very good, but when I'm bad, I'm better."
        -- Mae West

Alora

Of all the insufferable… "I think I know why they call you Rooster," I said.

"Why's that, sunshine?"

"Because you're randy like one." I moved closer. "Tell me I'm wrong."

He shook his head, his smile firmly in place. "You're not wrong. Or at least, back when I earned my name, that would have been a correct assumption. These days not so much. I've become a bit more discerning in my old age."

"Old age?" I looked him over from head to toe, trying real hard not to stare at the bulge behind his zipper. It was a little difficult to ignore since it wasn't exactly tiny. "You can't be older than your early thirties. That's hardly old."

"You certainly know how to flatter a man. But you're off on my age by a decade. I'm in my forties. I admit in my twenties and early thirties, I'd gladly screw any woman who lifted her skirt. Then I started wanting something more."

My jaw dropped as I stared at him. He seriously expected me to believe he was in his forties? No fucking way. I didn't see so much as one silver hair anywhere. Other than faint lines by his eyes, he didn't have a single wrinkle either. I couldn't decide if I was impressed, or jealous. My mother hadn't aged well, and I sometimes worried I'd end up looking old well before my time.

"Close your mouth, baby, or I'll think you want something in it." He smirked.

My gaze dropped to the bulge in his jeans again and I couldn't help but lick my lips. I didn't consider myself a whore by any means, but I had a healthy sexual appetite, and it had been far too long since my fling with Colorado. One-night stands tended to be too risky, so I avoided them if at all possible. Too many of my high school friends had been knocked up or caught something from the boys they'd slept with. It had made me a bit more cautious. Still, a girl had needs.

He took a step closer then another. He stopped inches from me, towering over my smaller frame. My breath caught and I realized I liked the way he made me feel. The sheer size of him didn't scare me. It turned me on. Knowing he was bigger, stronger, and could pin me down had me so incredibly wet.

"You want to play? Because I'm game if you are," he said.

"Play?" I asked.

He nodded. "Where are all the toys you've bought?"

I pointed up at the ceiling. "Bedroom. Including the batch that arrived today. I left some of them charging."

"You the type who says no but really means yes?" he asked.

I blinked trying to figure out what he meant. Didn't no always mean no?

He leaned closer, his nose brushing mine. "What I mean, baby girl, is if you tell me no do you really want me to stop, or do you want me to convince you that you want it? Is no for you a firm answer? Because I will *never* take what you don't offer. I need to be real clear on what you expect and want."

"Bunnies," I said.

"Bunnies?"

I nodded. "That's my safe word. If you do something that scares me, or if I feel things are going too far, I'll say bunnies."

"Then let the games begin." He grinned before tossing me over his shoulder. I gave a squeak as he smacked my ass, but it quickly turned to a moan when he slid his fingers under the leg of my shorts and felt just how much I wanted him. He rubbed up and down the lips of my pussy, his fingers barely brushing my clit before moving away.

"Rooster, I... Oh, God. I'm already close to coming."

"I'll make you come. You'll be screaming in pleasure, and after I've sated your most pressing needs, you're going to suck my cock." I wriggled on his shoulder, his words lighting a fire inside me. He smacked my ass again, harder this time. It burned and stung, but in the best of ways. "Hold still or you won't just be sucking it, kitten. I'll be fucking your throat and make you take every inch."

I closed my eyes, my nipples suddenly so hard they hurt. What the hell was this man doing to me? He had barely touched me and already I felt like I might combust. One thing was for certain. I'd never met a man like Rooster before, and I wasn't sure I ever would again. They'd broken the mold with him.

He went upstairs and moved down the hall to the open bedroom door. Tossing me onto the bed, he watched me bounce. Or more accurately, he watched my breasts bounce under my shirt. His cock seemed to grow even more as he stared at me. I pointed to the dresser, my hand shaking slightly.

"Those the new toys?" he asked.

"Yes."

"Where are the others?"

"Under the bed. There's a storage tub where I keep them." It had been designed for storing clothes, but I'd made it work for my needs. To ensure none of them were damaged, if the toys came in a box, I always put them back after I'd cleaned them. The rest I'd made little bags for out of silky material.

He pulled the long tub from under the bed and whistled as he lifted the lid and checked out the contents. "I'm not sure where to even start. You have quite the collection."

He removed a few items and set them aside. While he moved over to the dresser to check out my newest purchases, I reached into the bedside table for the bottle of lube. I didn't think we'd need any, since I'd never been so wet in my life, but I also didn't know what all he planned to do to me.

I saw the egg in his hand when we came back to the bed and butterflies erupted in my stomach. I'd been dying to try out the toy and it seemed I'd get my wish.

"It says there's an app for this thing," he said.

"You read the box?" I asked.

He nodded. "You left it out. I'm going to download it and let it sync while we play with some of these other things. Hope you don't have plans for the rest of the day."

I shook my head. Nope. Not a single plan at all, except to come as much as humanly possible. I'd thought I'd be getting myself off all day. Instead, I had a sexy biker willing to take on the task. It was like Christmas! Best present ever…

"Strip, unless you want me to tear those clothes off you," he said.

My eyes widened and my clit throbbed. Tear them... Holy hell! He arched an eyebrow when he realized I wasn't moving. He removed his cut and set it out of the way before tugging his shirt over his head. I didn't know how men did that. He'd grabbed the back of the neck and hauled it over his body. I'd always loved watching men do that, but with Rooster, it turned me on even more.

"Remember you were warned," he said. Rooster reached for me and ripped my shirt down the middle. He spread the material wide and cupped my breasts in his hands. "So fucking pretty. I can't wait to watch them bounce when I fuck you."

He tore my shorts from my body and placed his hands on the insides of my thighs, spreading me open. He picked up a length of material and I realized he'd found the blindfold inside the storage container.

"You trust me?" he asked.

I shouldn't. The man was a stranger. Then again, he knew the Devil's Fury and if they sent him to watch over me, I didn't think he'd hurt me. Not after the lengths they went to when my uncle had been murdering women. They'd tracked me down and made sure I was safe.

"I trust you," I said.

He tied the cloth over my eyes then I felt the hair on his chest rub against my nipples. I sucked in a breath and my toes curled as sparks shot from my breasts to my pussy. He did it again, and I nearly begged him to make me come.

"We're going to get the first one over with quick. I'll take my time with you after I've taken the edge off." He kissed my collarbone before backing away. I missed the heat of his body.

I heard the whir of one of the toys as he turned it

on. He slid the silicone up and down my pussy before parting the lips and touching it to my clit. I screamed and bucked, my orgasm hitting me fast and hard. He rubbed the small vibrator over the sensitive bud, wringing every drop of pleasure from my body. I felt my release soaking the bed under me.

"You're so damn pretty when you come." He turned the toy off. "Bet you'd be even prettier all tied up and completely at my mercy."

"Oh, God. Rooster! I…"

"You want that? Want me to tie you up?" he asked.

I nodded eagerly. It was one of the things I enjoyed most. I liked the complete submission. Knowing someone else was in control of my pleasure. Of my body. It heightened every sensation.

"You don't have the items I'd prefer to use, but we'll work with what you have. I'm going to move you to the center of the bed." He carefully lifted me and placed me where he wanted me. I heard the buckle on the leather cuffs I'd bought two years ago. He used them fasten my arms over my head and gripped my hips, tugging the rest of my body down so that I was stretched tight. "I'd tie your ankles too, but I want access to all of you."

I whimpered at the implication and wondered if I'd survive my day with Rooster. Worse, what would I do when he left? I had a feeling this one time with him would never be enough. I craved sex. Needed it like most people needed air. Using the toys brought me enough relief most of the time, but it wasn't the same as being with a man, especially one like Rooster.

"Before we go any further, just want you to know I'm clean. Get tested regular and haven't been with anyone since the last one. Anything you need to confess?" he asked.

"No, I'm clean. I haven't been with anyone since…"

"Colorado?" he asked.

I nodded. If the Devil's Fury had asked his club to watch over me, they'd likely mentioned my fling with Colorado too. The bikers were worse than gossiping old women.

"Then get ready to scream, sunshine. I'm about to blow your mind."

My heart hammered in my chest and I couldn't wait to see what he'd do or say next. The man was lethal. If he ever decided to work in the porn industry, he'd make a killing. Or better yet, he could sell fantasies to women and give them whatever they wanted most in the bedroom.

Oh, I need to remember that! Plot bunny!

I felt him slide the egg inside me. He tapped on something, most likely his phone, and it started up with a low vibration. It pulsed, pausing every few seconds before starting up again. He tugged the silicone string up through my pussy lips and placed the little rounded knob over my clit. I moaned and tugged at the bindings.

"You like having your ass played with?" he asked.

"Yes! Please, Rooster!"

"Want every hole filled?" he asked.

"God, yes!"

He chuckled, the sound dark and gritty. "Such a dirty little slut. Maybe I should have asked the auditor and cop to stick around. Is that your fantasy, Alora? You want more than one man fucking you at the same time?"

My heart took off at a gallop and my cheeks

burned with how easily he could read me. It was something I'd always wanted, but I'd never been brave enough to try. I wasn't sure I could handle more than one man at a time.

"Or maybe I should have just let them watch while I played with you." He stroked my nipples before giving them a pinch. "Would you like that? Having someone watch as I fuck you?"

"Yes, Rooster. I want that… I want… want…"

"Want what, kitten?" he asked, before lightly brushing his lips over mine.

"Use me. I want you to use me, and I want someone to watch."

He nuzzled my jaw. "That something you want right now? Because I can make it happen. I typically don't share, but if it makes you hot knowing someone is watching you get fucked, then I'll give you what you want."

"Please," I begged.

I heard him talk to someone called Samurai, inviting him into the house.

It wasn't long before the heavy tread of boots on the stairs could be heard from down the hall. The scent of sandalwood teased my nose when the other man entered the room.

"You sure about this, Rooster?" he asked, his voice pitched soft and low.

"She wants it. No touching. You can watch. If she asks for it, you can jerk off. But that's it." I felt the vibration of Rooster's growl. "And you damn sure forget what she looks like after this."

"You got it," Samurai answered.

"Baby girl, I'm removing your blindfold a moment so you can see who's here with us. All right?"

I nodded.

- 33 -

He untied the sash and I blinked to clear my vision. The man who'd joined us appeared younger than Rooster. I understood where his name came from when I saw him. He looked like he should be holding a Samurai sword and going into battle, his long hair braided and falling over his shoulder. His eyes seemed to look right through me.

"You good?" Rooster asked.

"Yes."

"I'm leaving the blindfold off a moment. Until I know you're comfortable with this." Rooster set the cloth aside and reached for one of the vibrating plugs. He used the lube to slick the silicone before placing it between my ass cheeks. I wiggled my hips, silently asking for more. He brought his hand down across my breast, leaving a stinging slap on my nipple. I gasped and arched my back. "Don't be trying to pull the toys into your gorgeous body. I'll give you what you want when I deem it's time."

"Yes, Rooster."

I looked over at Samurai and noticed he was getting hard. His gaze had locked onto my breasts and he let out a low growl when Rooster pinched my still aching nipple.

"What do you want, Alora?" Rooster asked. "Still want me to use you? Treat you like a whore?"

I jerked my gaze to him and saw the heat in his eyes. "Yes."

"Do you want Samurai to jerk off while he watches?" he asked.

I nodded my head.

Samurai unfastened his belt and jeans before pulling his cock out. He gave it a long, slow stroke and my pussy clenched with need.

"Such a dirty girl," Rooster murmured. "What

would you have done if I'd left the blindfold on until the end only for you to discover a room of men watching you?"

I tried to squeeze my thighs together, but he slapped the insides of them, pushing them apart again. He smacked my pussy and turned up the vibrations on the egg. I'd never been the type to bring home more than one man at a time, but his words and the image he'd planted in my head made me burn so hot.

"I think she likes that idea," Samurai said.

Rooster gripped my chin and forced me to hold his gaze. "You're mine, Alora. I'll let Samurai watch. Hell, if you want to get fucked in front of more of my brothers, I won't tell you no. But understand one thing. Your body is *mine*. No one fucks you but me. I find out anyone else touched you, put their cock in you, and there will be consequences."

"Rooster, I... what are you saying? This is just... just a onetime thing."

He shook his head. "Fuck no. I'm going to come down your throat. Come in your ass. Pound your pussy so good you can't sit for a week. I'm going to brand myself in your body, Alora. Colorado might have let you get away, but I'm not that fucking stupid."

"I don't understand," I said.

"He's claiming you." Samurai smirked as he tugged on his dick. "And I must say, I'm surprised he's willing to give you this much. Most of us are possessive bastards. Anyone even thought to look at Clarity with lust in their eyes and Scratch would blind them. Same goes for any other brother who has an old lady. He's giving you a gift."

"I won't belong to anyone," I said. "I'm *not* yours!"

Rooster growled. "Really? We'll see about that. Don't want to be mine? Only want a good hard fuck before you toss me out?"

He started to unfasten his pants and my heartrate shot through the roof. I didn't know what I'd just done, but I had a feeling it wasn't good. He wasn't just turned on anymore. No, he was pissed as hell. I'd unleashed something and I wasn't sure I could put the monster back into the box.

He tossed the plug to the side and lubed his fingers. His gaze was hot on mine as he worked first one finger then another into my ass. It stretched and burned, even though I'd already played back there earlier. By the time I was taking three fingers, I felt like a hot needy mess.

Rooster changed the setting on the egg again and I screamed and thrashed from the intense vibrations. He gripped my hips to hold me steady and I felt the head of his cock as he slowly pushed his way into my body. My ass hurt from the sheer size of him. Despite his anger, he took his time, working his cock into me one inch at a time. When I'd taken all of him, I could see the darkness in his eyes and knew I'd screwed up.

"Just a fuck?" he asked. "Don't want to be mine?"

"I-I-I don't belong to anyone." Why did the words sound so weak all of a sudden? I didn't want to be his. Right? I was a strong, independent woman and I didn't need a man.

His grip on my hips tightened as he pulled back then thrust forward. The egg seemed to change in tempo with every punishing push and pull of his cock. My nerve endings were lighting up. He fucked me hard and deep.

Oh, God! Maybe I do need him. Or at least his cock.

I came so hard I thought I might black out. Rooster changed his angle and rhythm, making the orgasm seem to last forever.

"Who do you belong to?" he asked.

"No one."

He rocked into me faster and it felt like his cock was swelling, becoming even larger than before. I yanked at the cuffs, my emotions on overload.

"Who. Do. You. Belong. To?" he asked, each word a near growl as he thrust into me.

"No one!" I screamed.

Rooster snarled and pulled free of my body, then finished himself off, spraying my stomach and breasts with his cum. His chest was heaving as he got off the bed. I looked to where Samurai had stood and found that he'd left at some point. I hadn't even noticed.

Rooster shoved his cock into his pants and fastened them before stomping out of my room. I cried out, worried he planned to leave me like this. My thoughts spun in a hundred different directions. When he returned a few minutes later, relief flooded me.

"You're an asshole," I muttered.

He didn't say a word, but he pulled the egg from my pussy and shut it off. He unfastened the cuffs and pulled me up into his arms, carrying me to the bathroom. As much as I wanted to push him away, I didn't have the energy to put up a fight. Rooster started the shower and set me under the warm spray. He stripped out of his clothes and joined me, pulling me against his chest.

He stroked my back and pressed a kiss to the top of my head. "Why didn't you say it?"

"Say what?"

"Bunnies. I kept thinking you'd use your safe word at any moment. Why didn't you?" he asked.

I pressed my face into his chest. I didn't know why I hadn't, except... I'd liked everything he'd done to me. Well, minus the part where he kept demanding I be his and only his. But the sex? It had easily been the best of my life. I liked how wild and untamed he'd seemed, even when he was trying to punish me for not giving him what he wanted.

"I'm not giving up, Alora. You're mine, whether you admit it or not."

"You don't even know me." We'd just met! I didn't understand his need to keep me, to make me his. Yeah, it sometimes worked like that in books and movies, but this was real life and not fiction.

"I know more than you think," he murmured. "There's not another woman like you in all the world. I refuse to let you walk away. I'll just have to prove to you that we're supposed to be together."

It would have been the sweetest words I'd ever heard, if I didn't think he was completely crazy for saying them to a woman he'd just met. Either way, I had to admit I liked having him around. At the very least, my dry spell would be over.

"If it includes more sex like what we just shared, then I'm game. Take as much time as you want to convince me."

He chuckled. "Remember you asked for it."

I had a feeling I was going to be incredibly sore, and I'd probably love every second of it. Too bad for Rooster I was stubborn as hell. Just because he wanted me to be his, didn't mean it would happen.

Chapter Four
"Sex pretty much cures everything."
-- Chuck Palahniuk

Rooster

Stubborn ass woman!

I leaned against my bike at the curb outside her house, ankles and arms crossed, as I tried to find a way back inside. After I'd held her most of last night, I'd decided to be nice and step out for breakfast while she slept. Imagine my surprise when she answered the door, snatched the box of donuts from my hand, and slammed the door in my face. I'd heard the lock twist into place and her snickering on the other side.

Good thing I thought she was so damn cute.

Celeste pulled into the drive, took one look at me, and burst out laughing. "I never thought I'd see the day you wanted a woman this bad."

I ignored her and kept watching for Alora. Every now and then, I'd see the curtains twitch. I knew damn well she was checking to see if I was still here. Celeste knocked on the door and tapped her foot while she waited. It only took a few minutes before Alora let her in. The feisty woman gave me a glare before slamming the door again.

Fuck this shit. I pushed away from my bike and went up to the house. I kept a lockpick set on me and pulled it out then set to work on her front door. It wasn't too difficult to open, and in less than a minute, I was letting myself in.

She poked her head out of her office and stared me down. "What the hell are you doing in my house?"

"Clearly I didn't do my job right and you need more orgasms because you're being a cranky little shit this morning."

She gasped and her eyes went wide. "I can't believe you just said that to me."

I heard Celeste laugh from inside the office. "Believe it. That one doesn't let anything stand in his way when he really wants something."

Alora glanced back into her office, her brow furrowed. "So what? I'm a game?"

"No." I strode forward and didn't stop until I was right in front of her. "You're not a fucking game, Alora. You may have only met me yesterday, but I've been watching over you for weeks. I know your favorite foods, favorite wine, the types of books you write, and the ones you read. I know you like romantic comedies as much as you like action films where they blow shit up every fifteen minutes."

"Stalker!"

I pinched the bridge of my nose. "I'm not a fucking stalker. I was making sure you were safe. Jesus. This is why I'm still single."

"As much fun as it is to watch the two of you circle one another, can this wait, Rooster? I need to get the files and books from her so I can drop them with the auditor."

"You're done?" I asked, holding Alora's gaze.

"Mostly. There's still a few I need to track down and bookmark, but I thought he could get started on what I'd put together so far."

"You need to work the rest of the day?" I asked.

She nodded. "I'm seriously behind on my deadline, and I still need to finish finding the scenes in my books for the auditor."

I rubbed my hand along my jaw. "How about this. I'll have Chinese delivered and while you work on your new book, you give me a list of what needs to be found for the auditor. I can work on that while you get caught up."

She blinked at me a moment. "You want to read my books and find scenes where my character talks about, reviews, or uses sex toys? You realize I wrote romances, right?"

I leaned in, dropping my voice so Celeste wouldn't hear. "Honey, I've read all of them. Bought them online and read them on my phone over the last few weeks."

Her gaze softened and she nibbled her bottom lip. "Really?"

I nodded.

"All right. I'd love your help." She smiled softly. "And Chinese would be great. As long as there are lots of egg rolls. Those are the best part."

"You got it. Tons of egg rolls."

She moved closer and pressed a kiss to my cheek. "Thanks, Rooster. No one's ever offered to do something like this for me. It means a lot."

Celeste poked her head out of the office. "None for me. As soon as she hands me everything, I'm out of here. Besides, I have a hot date tonight."

"Wouldn't by any chance be with Phantom, would it?" I asked.

She lifted her chin and stared down her nose at me. "Like I'd tell you."

Yeah, that pretty much was answer enough. She'd been tailing him for a while now. I wondered if Phantom had any idea what he was getting himself into with that one. Even if he did age well, I knew the bastard had to be fifty by now, if not older. Celeste wasn't exactly fresh out of high school, but I knew she was only in her twenties. Then again, everyone in the club seemed to pair up with younger women. If I ever got Alora to stop giving me shit and let me claim her, I'd be following the same path.

I let Alora and Celeste finish up while I placed the food order. I remembered Alora not having much in her fridge, so I shot off a text to a Prospect.

Putting in a grocery order. I'll forward you the info. Pick it up and drop by Alora's place.

I got a thumbs up emoji in response and opened the grocery app on my phone. I put in all the basics I thought Alora should have in her kitchen, added a case of beer on the off chance she let me stick around this time, and a few easy dinner options. Once I had the order number and pick-up time, I sent the info to the Prospect.

"Don't suppose you want some wine?" Alora asked.

"Nope. I ordered some sodas and beer in addition to the Chinese."

"Are you sure you want to do this?" she asked. "Because I'll understand if you changed your mind."

I tugged her against me, placing my hand at her waist. "I wouldn't have offered if I didn't want to actually help."

"When you said you knew me... it was because you've been following me on social media and reading my books, wasn't it?"

I shrugged. "Partly. Charming asked me to keep an eye on you after we found out you were in the area. I paid attention."

She rubbed her hands up and down my chest, leaning into me. As much as I wanted to kiss her, I also worried it might make her bolt. I'd come on too strong yesterday, and now I needed to do some damage control.

"You're different from the men I've known," she

said.

"In a good way I hope."

She nodded. "Definitely in a good way. I'm not ready to be yours though, Rooster. There's so much I want to see and do. I don't want to settle down with anyone. Not for a while."

"Why don't you let me try to convince you?" I asked. "Might be fun. I can show you all the benefits of being mine."

"Name one."

I leaned down until our noses nearly touched. "Lots of orgasms."

She snorted then giggled. "All right. Fair point. But I need more than that out of a relationship, Rooster."

"Do you agree to keep an open mind?" I asked.

She drew back and eyed me. "Fine. I'll keep an open mind. But that's all I'm promising."

Even if it wasn't quite what I'd hoped for, it did give me an opening. Little did Alora realized what she'd agreed to. I planned to do everything in my power to make sure she agreed to being my old lady before it was all said and done. While she was beautiful, I was drawn to her for more than that. Her words had lured me in. The pictures she painted in her books had made me laugh, definitely made me hard, and the sappy endings had made me smile.

I enjoyed her wit, and even liked the bit of verbal sparring we'd done so far. I knew there would never be a dull moment with her around. It was hard to picture her as being related to Twister. I'd heard plenty about him and knew exactly why he'd been exiled from the Devil's Fury. Alora seemed to be the opposite of her uncle. If there was meanness inside her, I hadn't witnessed it yet. In fact, I'd watched her give up her place in line to a woman with small children, let an elderly lady take a parking space Alora had been waiting for, and even offer some money to a child who wanted to buy their mother a present. She might be feisty with me, but I'd seen her kindness.

I followed her to the office, and she handed me the receipts she hadn't paired with books yet. I recognized a few of the items from the book I'd read last week, so I started there. She handed me a paperback of each title and I got to work tracking down the passages. Alora gave me post-it flags to mark each page and I noted the page numbers for the various items on the receipts. The doorbell rang about twenty minutes into our work, and I got up to answer it.

"I can get it," she said, starting to rise from her desk.

"Stay and work on your book. It's probably our lunch. Do you want to take a break and eat or have lunch at your desk?"

"I typically eat in here when I'm on a deadline."

"All right. I'll be back in a minute." I smiled as she went right back to typing. At some point, she'd pulled up her hair with a clip and a few strands had escaped and hung in wisps near her face. Adorable.

The doorbell chimed again, and I went to answer it. I yanked it open, expecting to find a Prospect on the porch. Instead, I found Officer Murray. I narrowed my eyes and held back a growl. What the fuck was he doing here?

He scowled when he saw me. "Why are you here?"

I snorted. "I was just thinking the same about you."

"I came to check on Miss Danvers."

"Yeah, I just bet you did. Alora is fine. She's working."

He frowned. "Then why are you here? Doesn't she need to focus or something?"

"I'm helping her." I grinned. Let him make of that what he would. Asshole didn't need to know I was marking passages of books for the auditor. For all he knew, I was here to inspire her. Although, I wouldn't mind doing a bit of that too. "You've done your job, *Officer*. Alora is perfectly fine. Now, leave."

I shut the door in his face and twisted the lock to be sure he wouldn't let himself in. I couldn't stand the pompous ass. Officer Murray didn't realize I knew all about him. The local police had a few corrupt officers, and the chief could be bought with enough cash or donations, like the bulletproof vest we got for the department's K-9 officer. Thanks to the generosity of the Devil's Boneyard, the chief looked away on the small stuff. But the shit Officer Murray was into wasn't something the club would ever condone. These days, we weren't into the heavy shit anymore. Too many families in the club now.

"Rooster," Alora called out.

I went to check on her and came to a halt in the doorway. "Why are you standing on your chair?"

"Spider!" She pointed at the floor. "I felt it crawl over my foot. Oh, God! I need a shower. And bug spray! Lots and lots of bug spray."

I rolled my lips into my mouth and bit down so I wouldn't laugh. I knelt on the floor and checked under her desk. If there was a spider, it had moved on. I didn't think she wanted to hear that though. As much as I hated crawling around the floor, I checked the area as best I could. Until I noticed a daddy long-legs on the wall just above the baseboard behind her chair.

"Don't move, baby girl."

"You found it?" she asked.

"Yep." I reached over and got the spider onto my hand then stood and carried it to the front door. I tossed it out into the yard and hoped it didn't come back inside. I had a feeling Alora would demand it be killed next time.

"Wash your hands," she yelled out. "Twice!"

I chuckled and used her hall bathroom to wash up. When I'd finished, there was a knock at the door. I hoped like hell Officer Murray wasn't back. I was glad as fuck it was Carlos on the doorstep.

"Picked up your food and the grocery order. Where do you want everything?" he asked.

"Put the groceries on the kitchen counter and lunch on the table."

"Want me to put the cold stuff in the fridge?" he asked.

"Yeah and toss out anything expired. I don't know how the woman has survived this long."

"You got it, Rooster."

I put Gypsy out back so I wouldn't have to worry about the kid letting her out. I went back to Alora's office to see if I could pry her away from her book. Her glasses had slid down her nose and she had her bottom lip clamped between her teeth. Her fingers flew so fast over the keys, it sounded like gunfire. I leaned against the doorframe and watched her a moment.

"Lunch is here. I'll bring you a plate in a minute."

She stopped mid-keystroke and looked up. "Lunch?"

I shook my head. "Yeah, baby girl. Lunch. Remember, you asked for egg rolls?"

"Oh! That sounds good. See if they gave us duck

- 46 -

sauce. I like to pour it over my egg rolls. And soy sauce for the rice please."

Before I could respond she was back to typing. I went to the kitchen and started pulling out the cartons of Chinese food and sorting everything. Carlos finished putting the cold stuff in the fridge and let himself out. It was no secret I had a thing for the sexy author, but I had a feeling he'd be blabbing the second he got back to the clubhouse. Wanting in her pants, and playing house were two different things. Me calling dibs on her and deciding to keep her weren't the same.

I piled five egg rolls on her plate, along with some fried rice and orange chicken. I dug through the kitchen drawers until I found a fork and got one of the sodas from the fridge. I carried her lunch to her office and set it on her desk before going back to fix mine. If she planned to eat in there, then I would too.

I let Gypsy back in and tossed her a rib bone from the large bag Alora had in the pantry. She carried it off to her bed in the living room, and I hoped she'd stay occupied for a while.

I settled back in the chair I'd used while looking up the passages of her books and kicked my feet out, crossing them at the ankles. I leaned back and dug into my food. Chinese food was my downfall. And tacos. I could eat both almost daily and never get tired of them. Of course, if I did that, I'd end up being soft and round. Last time I checked, the ladies tended to prefer my six pack. Alora certainly hadn't complained last night.

"Oh. My. God." She moaned and my dick went hard as granite. "This is so amazing."

I looked over and saw her bite into an egg roll, her eyes closed and a look of pure bliss on her face. Maybe I could win her over with food and orgasms.

Although, the way she was going after that egg roll, and the noises she was making, made me wonder if she was going to orgasm over her food.

"I think I'm jealous," I said.

Her eyes popped open. "Of what?"

"That egg roll. You sound like you're seconds from coming."

Her cheeks went pink, and her lips tipped up on one corner. "Maybe I am. But you don't need to be jealous. You were better than the egg roll."

"Good to know. In that case, maybe you'd like to head upstairs later. You still have a lot of toys I haven't had a chance to play with."

"Upstairs?" she asked, her mouthful of egg roll.

"Unless you've met your quota on orgasms for the week."

She swallowed hard and coughed as she choked on her food. She patted her chest and sucked in a deep breath. "Really?"

"Only if you want to."

She nodded eagerly. "I want to. I really, really want to. I haven't written this much in… forever. I think the sex last night rewired my brain or something. I'll take as many orgasms as you want to give me. It's been a while."

At least I now knew the secret to getting Alora right where I wanted her. Ply her with food and orgasms, and just maybe she'd be mine by end of the week. At the very least, I'd enjoy every second of our time together. I'd take what I could get.

For the moment.

Chapter Five

"Sex is not the answer. Sex is the question. 'Yes' is the answer."

-- Swami X

Alora

I fanned myself as I watched Rooster. He'd made it through the rest of the receipts, and we'd handed off the books and list to Celeste after lunch. Now he'd kicked back in my reading chair and had grabbed my latest book. It wasn't technically available yet, but I had a box of review copies to send to bloggers, newspapers, and libraries in hopes of generating some buzz before it released. Why was it so sexy that he not only read my books but enjoyed them?

I kept trying to push him away, then he'd do something amazing like order me a bunch of egg rolls and promise multiple orgasms. To actually see him enjoying my work was a big turn on too. So far, Rooster was unlike the other bikers I'd met. Colorado had been fun, but I'd seen the darkness in his eyes. I'd known the men of the Devil's Fury could be violent. Either Rooster's club was different, or he hid that part of himself pretty well.

I honestly didn't know anything about him. He hadn't discussed himself at all. I saved my file and shut down my computer. I'd spent the last fifteen minutes watching him instead of working. There wasn't much point in trying to do anything else for the day. Besides, I'd gotten a lot accomplished. I might not be caught up, but I was well on the way to digging myself out of the hole I'd created.

"You done?" he asked, not even looking up from the page he was reading.

"For today. So, can we talk a minute?"

He lowered the book. "That sounds ominous."

"You said you wanted to claim me. I learned all about being the property of a biker when I was with the Devil's Fury. Why should I even consider something like that when I don't know anything about you?"

He grunted and set the book side, folding his arms over his broad chest. "I guess that's a fair point. You can ask me ten questions, but I can't promise I'll be able to answer them all."

I'd take what I could get. The man was already working his way past my defenses. I didn't know why him of all people. Why couldn't I have felt this way about Officer Murray? I might have let the cop into my bed for one night, if Rooster hadn't come along. The moment I'd seen him, I'd lost interest in Officer Murray. So if I was only going to get ten questions, I needed to make them count.

"I'm guessing you aren't from Florida. Not with your accent," I said.

His lips twitched like he fought back a smile. "My family is from Ireland. Moved to this country when I was young and made my way to Florida in my late teens."

Ireland. I'd thought that was the accent I'd heard. Why did that make him even sexier? If I'd hoped the allure of Rooster would dim the more I knew about him, so far it was backfiring. One question down. Nine to go.

"Why did you join the Devil's Boneyard?" I asked.

"I met a few clubs before I came to Florida. None of them felt like a good fit. I hung around town and saw the Devil's Boneyard. I watched and waited. After a few weeks, I approached Cinder. The rest, as they say, is history."

I wondered if he'd give me a straight answer if I asked if he'd ever killed anyone. For that matter, did I really want to know? What if he'd had a good reason? Men who walked the straight and narrow killed people in the line of duty. Guys in the military killed during war. Police sometimes had to kill in order to protect the community. It didn't make them bad people. Even if Rooster had killed someone, it didn't mean he was a bad guy. Better work my way up to that one.

"Are your parents alive? Or do you have any family in the US?" I asked.

The light dimmed in his eyes and his jaw hardened. "My father wasn't a nice man. Got mixed up in shit back in Ireland. My family came here for a fresh start, but that only works if your father isn't a dumbass. He didn't learn his lesson and double-crossed some dangerous men. It ended up getting him killed, as well as my mother. I doubt I have any family left in Ireland. I've stayed under the radar so those bastards won't come after me. Not too long ago, someone said I had a half-brother. Supposedly my mother cheated on my father. We decided to have one of those DNA tests done. Turns out the guy was wrong. We aren't related."

My eyes went wide. "You think they're still looking for you? You were just a kid!"

"You don't walk away from the Irish mob, Alora. They wanted to wipe out my entire line. I was fifteen at the time. Old enough to cause trouble for them. I spent years hiding and doing my best to not draw attention to myself. When Cinder let me prospect for the club, he offered me his protection. Now I have an entire club of brothers at my back. I doubt the mob would try anything, even if they did find me."

I didn't even know what to say to him. He'd lost his family and had run for his life. I couldn't imagine what it was like to be on the run at such a young age. Somehow, he'd survived and turned into a rather remarkable man, from what I'd seen so far. I got up and went to him, sitting across his lap. I reached up and cupped his cheek.

"You're rather amazing. You know that?"

He smiled and tugged me closer, pressing his lips to mine. "No, *a ghrá*. You're the one who's remarkable."

"What does that mean? You've called me that twice now."

He arched an eyebrow. "Sure you want to use up one of your questions?"

I hesitated, but decided I needed to know. The way he looked at me when he said it... "I'm sure."

"It means love. Never used it with another woman. You're the first and I'm hoping you'll be the last."

And that was the moment the walls around my heart cracked. If anyone could convince me to give them a shot at forever, it was Rooster. No one had ever been so sweet to me. So charming.

"So you earned the name Rooster fair and square?" I asked.

He cleared his throat and looked away a moment. I didn't think he'd answer me. When his gaze clashed with mine, I saw resolve in the greenish depths. "I haven't exactly been a monk, Alora. I won't lie about my past. I've had more than my share of women. When I first started to prospect for the club, I wasn't all that discerning about where I put my dick. The club decided to make sure I never forgot about it."

"In case you didn't notice, I wasn't a virgin last night. I can't very well hold your past against you when I've been with other men. Besides, it's not like we knew each other. Even if we had, you probably lost your virginity before I was even born."

He placed a hand over his heart. "Ouch. You know where to hit a guy and make it hurt."

I rolled my eyes. "Yes, because you're ancient. Please! You're sexy and you damn well know it. Do you think I'd ever give a guy my age a shot? Let me assure you the answer is no. I need someone who has their shit together."

"Understandable. According to your biography in your books, you've hit a few bestseller lists. The big ones. I doubt you did that without putting in a lot of work. You've accomplished more in twenty years than most people will do in their entire lives."

"Twenty-one." I toyed with the edge of his cut. "My birthday was last week."

His brow furrowed. "How the hell did I miss that?"

"Stalker," I said, singing the word out.

"Careful or I'll spank your ass."

My breath caught and I pressed my thighs together. Spank me? Yes, please! The hard ridge of his cock under my ass told me enough. I wasn't the only one turned on by the thought of a spanking. *Focus, Alora!*

"I still have five questions left."

"Guess you better get to it. Otherwise, you may have to hold them for another day."

"Why?"

He grinned and pressed his cock against me. "I thought it was rather obvious. If you're telling me you didn't notice, my ego might take a big hit."

I leaned closer. "Does your ego need a bit of… stroking?"

"Oh, baby girl. You can stroke me anytime you want."

"You're terrible," I murmured, kissing his cheek, his jaw, and the side of his neck.

"That's not what you said last night. In fact, I think you called me God a few times."

"Are you sure I didn't call you Hades?"

"Pretty sure you screamed *oh, God*."

"Well, he's the god of the underworld." I smiled. "With your particular talents, I don't think you're from heaven."

"So you think I'm a sinner and not a saint?" he asked.

"Definitely a sinner."

He kissed my shoulder and rubbed the bristles on his chin against me. "Want to go sin with me?"

I rubbed my nose against his. "Who said we had to go anywhere before we sinned?"

He growled and tugged my shirt over my head. "Then you're wearing far too many clothes."

I stood and quickly stripped. Rooster shrugged out of his cut and gently set it on top of my swag organizer before pulling off his shirt. I froze, staring at the expanse of his chest. I'd always had a thing for men with wide chests and broad shoulders. And his biceps… if I'd been wearing panties, they'd be damp. Even though I'd seen him last night, in the light of day, he looked even more spectacular.

"I think I owe you a spanking for being such a smart ass," he said, tugging me across his thighs. His hand ran over my ass cheeks. "How many do you think you've earned?"

"Lots of them." I squirmed on his lap. The

anticipation was almost as good as the burn of a good spanking.

"Your fair skin will pink up so nicely. You still want to use bunnies for your safe word? I don't ever want to take things too far with you."

"Bunnies," I confirmed. Not that I thought I'd be using it. Today or any other day.

His hand cracked against my ass and I yelped, my feet kicking. He rubbed away the sting before landing another blow. By the fourth one, my skin burned, and my pussy was dripping wet. Rooster slid his finger between my legs and stroked me. The light brush of his fingertips against my clit had me crying out and so close to coming.

"Jesus. You're responsive as fuck, Alora."

"Rooster, please!"

"You need to come, baby girl?"

"Yes! Yes, Rooster. Make me come!"

He gripped my hair and turned my face so he could hold my gaze. "What if I tell you the only way you're coming is on my cock?"

I wanted that, so much. Wanted *him*. "Yes."

He lifted me so that I straddled him. "Bare?"

"I-I'm on birth control." Even though I'd been on the pill since I'd turned fifteen, I'd never let anyone fuck me without a condom before. I didn't know why I trusted him, but I did.

"And we already covered the part where we're both clean. So what's it going to be, beautiful?"

I swallowed hard. "I want you."

He unfastened his pants and freed his cock. My mouth watered as he gave it a few strokes. I wanted to taste him, to have him come on my tongue, but right now I needed him inside me. I lifted my hips and lowered myself on his hard shaft.

His jaw tightened and his eyes went dark. "You feel like fucking heaven."

"I'm no angel, Rooster."

He nipped my bottom lip. "Call me Killian."

"Killian."

He gripped my hips tight and stood, keeping himself buried inside me as he walked to the nearest bare wall. He pressed me back against it and I turned my head, noticing we were in plain view of the window.

"That's right, beautiful. Anyone looking will see me fucking you." He nipped me again before kissing me hard. "You like that, don't you? The thought of people watching you get fucked?"

"You know I do."

His driving thrusts made me see stars as he pounded into me. I didn't know if the thought of someone watching us turned him on too, or if it was something else lighting him on fire.

"I'll never share you. Don't even fucking ask me to." He kissed me, his tongue delving into my mouth.

I sank my nails into his shoulders. I couldn't even respond. He hit just the right spot and I came so hard I could feel the wetness on my thighs. Rooster slammed into me harder and let out a roar as he came, pumping a load of cum into me. He pressed tight against me and I felt the jerk of his cock. His chest heaved as he panted for breath.

Gypsy howled from somewhere in the house and my cheeks warmed. At least she hadn't barged in on us.

"That was an appetizer," he said.

"You're really okay with someone watching us?" I asked, thinking of Colorado and his comments about how possessive men like him were. Was Rooster not the same?

"Honestly, I'd prefer to have you all to myself, but if it's something you need, I'm not going to deny you. As long as no one else touches you."

"Have you ever been to The Black Rose?" I asked.

"The sex club?"

I nodded. "They supposedly have rooms with that two-way glass stuff. You know, like in the cop shows. You can't see who's on the other side, but anyone could watch you while you're in the rooms. I've never had anyone to go with, and I'm not sure I'd trust a stranger I met there. I'm only going off what I've read."

"That what you want? To go to The Black Rose?"

I trailed my finger over his collarbone. "Could be fun."

"I'll schedule something for tonight. As long as you realize I'm only doing this for you. Anyone else ever asked me for something like this, I'd have laughed in their face and told them to fuck off."

I cupped my hand behind his neck and kissed him softly. "Thank you, Killian."

"We go there and you only call me Sir the entire time. Got it?"

A slight smile curved my lips. "Yes, Sir."

Chapter Six
"Once you finish having sex, what is there to do but start over?"
-- Jarod Kintz

Rooster

I couldn't believe I'd agreed to this shit. Even at the clubhouse, I'd not felt right taking the club whores out in the open. But Alora got off on it. I'd packed a bag of toys, not trusting anything they kept in the rooms. They claimed the cost of the room included a selection of new toys you could take with you when you left. I'd selected a flogger, paddle, blindfold, and gag. Everything else I'd chosen from Alora's collection.

While she changed in the bathroom, I got everything set up. To make sure I wasn't recognized, I would be keeping my long-sleeve tee on, as well as my jeans and boots. I'd left my cut in my saddlebags. Alora would have a blindfold to hide part of her face, but I'd donned a plain black mask that covered everything from my hairline to the tip of my nose.

She stepped out of the bathroom in a black, silky negligee that left little to the imagination, but that was the point. Lace cupped her breasts letting the darkness of her nipples show. Christ! She damn near made my heart stop she was so fucking sexy. I'd never met anyone like her.

"Ready?" I asked.

"Yes, Sir."

Fuck! My dick went hard at her words. This was either going to be a really long hour, or it was going to pass too fast.

"What's your safe word?" I asked.

"Bunnies." She smiled at me, her eyes twinkling.

"Come here, gorgeous. I'm going to blindfold you then I'll open the curtains. Anything off limits?"

She shook her head.

"You want pleasure, pain, and to be shown off like a little whore?"

Her hands curled into fists and she licked her lips. "You know I do."

I tugged her closer and kissed her. "My dirty girl."

I placed the blindfold over her eyes and led her over to a padded bench. It faced the window and had an O-ring on the back where I could attach handcuffs or rope to tie her down. I pressed the button to open the curtains then made her kneel on the bench. I walked around so that I faced her. "Give me your hands, Princess."

"Yes, Sir." She held them out over the back of the padded leather.

I snapped a pair of cuffs on her and secured them to the ring. I took down the leather paddle I'd purchased with the room and braced my feet shoulder width apart. I smacked the paddle against my hand and heard her breath catch.

"You've been a bad girl, haven't you?"

"Yes, Sir. So bad."

"Count out your spankings, Princess. Anything other than the correct count slips past your lips, and you'll be punished. Understood?"

"Yes, Sir."

I swung the paddle, connecting over her negligee with a sharp smack.

"One, Sir."

I swung again.

"Two, Sir."

I added a little more power to the next one and

she yelped.

"Now what did I say, Princess? That didn't sound like you counting."

"Sorry, Sir."

"Bad girls get disciplined." I lifted the hem of the black silk over her ass. "Spread your legs, Princess. Let everyone see that pretty pink pussy."

She parted her thighs, and I brought my hand down on her ass. "Wider! I want to see those lips part."

She shuddered as she obeyed. She was pink and swollen, and oh so wet. Looked like my sweet Alora was enjoying herself. My cock was painfully hard, but I wasn't about to get off just yet.

I spanked her with the paddle again.

"Three, Sir."

The next swat left a red mark.

"Four, Sir!"

"One more, Princess. Be a good girl and count." I swung the paddle again.

"Five, Sir!"

"Is your ass nice and sore, Princess?"

She whimpered and nodded.

"I can't hear you."

"Yes, Sir. Hurts so good."

I spread her cheeks and dribbled lube down the crack. "It's about to hurt even more. I have something special for you today."

I took out the large anal vibrator and slicked it with lubricant before pressing the tip against her tight hole. I eased it inside her then used the remote to turn it on. I turned it on high and smiled as her back bowed and she cried out. Her thighs were slick, and I could smell her arousal.

"Let's give the nice people a show, Princess. You ready to come?"

"Yes, Sir! Please!"

I took out the largest vibrator she'd had and turned it on. It was shaped like a real cock, veins and all, and had to be over two inches in diameter. It was almost the same size as mine, but I was an inch longer. I plunged the toy inside her and worked it in and out of her pussy with quick hard strokes. She yanked at the cuffs, her body twisting and bucking. Her pussy gushed when she came, coating my hand and the toy in her release.

I pushed another button on the window remote, one she hadn't known about. It lit up the glass so I could see who stood on the other side. Three men in suits were sporting wood, and a woman who was twisting her nipples as she watched.

"Does my princess want her audience to come too?" I asked.

"Yes, Sir."

I gave the people on the other side of the window a nod. "You heard her gentlemen and lady. Get yourselves off and we'll give you an even better show."

The woman lifted her skirt and touched herself and the men freed their cocks, stroking them. I turned back to Alora and worked her pussy with the vibrator again. After she came twice more, I set the toy aside.

"Princess, I need you to lift up. I want those perky tits over the top of the bench. Let me see them."

"Yes, Sir." She shifted until her ribs were braced against the padded back and her breasts were in clear view.

I hit another button on the remote and the floor began to rotate, turning the bench clockwise. Time for the finale, then I wanted my girl all to myself. I ripped the lace covering her breasts and pinched her nipples.

She cried out, thrusting them into my hands. I attached vibrating nipple clamps to each side, tightening them until I heard her whimper.

"Are they throbbing?" I asked.

"Yes, Sir."

"Good." I turned the clamps on and leaned down so only she could hear me. "Your audience has gotten themselves off, but they're still watching."

I reached for the bag and took out the last item I'd packed. I turned it on so that it not only vibrated but heated up too. I slipped the thicker part inside her pussy until it pressed against her G-spot and the other half covered her clit.

"Oh, God! Oh… I… I…"

"Don't you dare fucking come until I'm inside you!"

"Y-Yes, S-Sir. I… I can't…"

She screamed as she came, and I knew I'd have to play to our audience and punish her again. I took the flogger off the wall and twisted my wrist in a figure eight to judge the weight and feel of it. I flogged her breasts until the skin turned pink, but the little minx came again during her punishment.

"Princess, what am I ever going to do with you?" I asked.

"Please, Sir. I need you."

"You need me?" I asked.

"Yes, Sir. Inside me. I ache."

"You ache." I used the flogger on her pussy, making her yelp in surprise. "Is this where you ache?"

"Yes, Sir!" She screamed out her answer as I continuously flogged her. When she was panting and I could tell she was seconds from breaking, I tossed it aside and unfastened my pants. I pulled out my cock and removed the toy in her ass.

"You don't come until I say you can. Understood?"

"Yes, Sir."

I slid my cock along the lips of her pussy, getting wet enough I wouldn't hurt her. Then I spread her ass cheeks wide and slowly pushed inside her. Once she'd taken all of me, I knew I couldn't hold back. We were both too close already. I took her with long, deep strokes, her breasts bouncing with every drive of my cock.

"You like that don't you? My dirty little whore likes having my dick in her ass."

"Yes! Yes, Sir. Oh, God. Please…"

I gripped her hips and chased my orgasm, knowing she was seconds from coming. When I felt my balls draw up and the tingle in my spine, I gave the command.

"Come for me, Princess. Come right fucking now!"

She screamed as she came, her body twitching from the intensity. I came inside her, not stopping until every last drop had been wrung from my balls. I glanced at the window and damn near lost my shit. The businessmen and woman were gone. In their place was none other than Officer Murray. Fucking asshole!

The way he grinned, he knew exactly who we were, and I didn't like the way he watched my woman. Not even a little. The lust in his eyes was different from the others. He wasn't just enjoying the show. No, he had plans for my sweet Alora. I didn't know what he was up to, but I'd find out. I didn't trust him. I dimmed the window and closed the curtain before I removed the toys, handcuffs, and blindfold.

She sagged against me and I lifted her into my arms. I carried her to the whirlpool tub in the bathroom and filled it with steamy water. I added some scented beads and rose petals from a set of jars on the ledge by the tub. Then I sank into the water with her in my arms. I cradled her against me, running my hand down her hair.

"You did good, baby girl. You were amazing."

"I've never..." She stopped and licked her lips. "It's never been like that. I feel... too much."

"Shh. Just relax, Alora. I've got you."

"Killian."

I kissed her brow. "Not now, angel. Just close your eyes and focus on breathing. Deep breath in and slowly release."

I ran my hands over her body in soothing strokes. She wasn't the only one on emotional overload right now. While I was pissed about Officer Murray, what we'd just shared in the other room was beyond anything I'd ever experienced before. I'd known she was one in a million.

"I'm never letting you go," I murmured. "You're mine, beautiful."

"Not property," she said, her voice drowsy and her speech slightly slurred.

"Oh, baby girl. It's not me who owns you. It's *you* who owns *me*. You've had me by the balls since the moment I stepped inside your house. There isn't a damn thing I wouldn't do for you."

Her fingers curled and she cuddled against me. "I'm scared, Killian. What if I can't handle all this? I've never really had a relationship. Not like this one."

"Let me share something with you, Alora. I've never had a serious girl or woman. Not when I was a kid and not in more recent years. I've chased a few, but never spent more than a week or two with them. With you, I want forever. I want to be the only one giving you orgasms. The one who falls asleep holding you at night. The guy lucky enough to wake up with you in his arms.

"I can't say the Irish mob will never come for me, but if they do, or anyone else tries to take you from me, I will defend you with my life. I will tear apart anyone who ever hurts you. And if I'm the one who causes you pain, you have my permission to tie me up and torture me."

"Killian." She lifted her head and I saw the tears in her eyes. "You really mean all that?"

I nodded. "Every word."

"But we just met. It's too soon!"

I cupped her cheek. "Baby girl, sometimes you just know. When it's right, it doesn't matter if a few hours have passed or a few years. You were mine before we ever spoke to one another. Then you opened that sassy mouth of yours and I wanted you even more."

She smiled and kissed me softly. "You like it when I'm sassy."

"Mmm. I do. It also makes me want to put something in your mouth, and I don't mean a lollipop."

She giggled and settled against me again. I wasn't sure if she'd just agreed to let me claim her, or if I'd have a fight on my hands again later. But for now, I felt content. Alora was in my arms, where she belonged. Nothing else mattered.

Chapter Seven
"Sex is like money; only too much is enough."
-- John Updike

Alora

It seemed my fight with the auditor wasn't over, but I'd officially hired Celeste to handle the issue. With her on my side, I had no doubt I'd win. It freed up my time to focus on my book, and a certain biker I couldn't get out of my thoughts. He'd gone back to his house the morning after we'd gone to The Black Rose, and I hadn't seen him since. Part of me worried something was wrong, or that I'd done or said something I shouldn't have, but I tried not to dwell on it. A few days had crawled by, then a week, and another. Now, nearly three weeks later, I wasn't sure if I should be concerned or moving on with my life.

I placed a hand over my belly. No, *our* lives. I'd missed my period five days ago and taken a home pregnancy test. After a freak out, I'd called my doctor to have the test confirmed. I'd forgotten about the antibiotics he'd given me about ten days before I met Rooster. It had made my birth control pills ineffective.

Even with the news swirling in my brain, I'd stopped myself from tracking him down. I'd finished all but the last three chapters of my novel, scrubbed my house from top to bottom, and taken Gypsy to the doggy salon. She hadn't been too thrilled with the pink bow they'd put on her and had taken to nipping my calves every time I walked by her. I was so unappreciated! At least her fur was silky and soft, even if she didn't care.

"Fuck it," I muttered. If Rooster wouldn't come to me, then I'd go to him. I glanced down at my around-the-house clothes and grimaced. Right after I changed.

I ran upstairs to shower and pulled on a pair of cut off shorts and a tank. Before I left the house, I made sure Gypsy ran to the bathroom and let her back in, double checking the lock on the door. I gave her a kiss on the head and grabbed my purse and keys. After I slipped on my Converse, I ran to my car. I didn't know what the hell I'd tell Rooster when I got there, but I was done sitting around not knowing where we stood. Did he want me or not?

Our last night together, he'd talked about keeping me forever. So why the sudden vanishing act? I didn't know if I should be afraid something happened to him, or if he was just ghosting me. I wouldn't leave the Devil's Boneyard compound without answers. Even if it meant sitting outside the gates in my car until someone talked to me.

I pulled onto the two-lane highway and headed for the edge of town. About a mile from the turnoff to the compound, I saw blue flashing lights behind me. A quick glance at my speedometer had me cursing. I hadn't even realized I was speeding. Just what I needed, a fucking ticket. I pulled to the side of the road, rolled down my window, and made sure my insurance and driver's license was within reach. Then I placed my hands on the steering wheel and waited.

Officer Murray leaned down and peered into my window, and down the front of my shirt. *Pervert.* He lowered his sunglasses and grinned.

"Well, well. Miss Danvers, where are you off to in such a hurry?"

"Just going to see someone. I'm really sorry. I didn't realize I was speeding."

Officer Murray tapped my door. "You know,

there's no reason for me to write you a ticket. It would make your insurance go up and cause you a hassle."

"Really? You'll let me off with a warning?"

He smiled, but there was something off about it. "Of course! I'll do a favor for you as long as you do something for me."

The hair on my nape stood up. I didn't like where this was going. How had I found him charming when he'd shown up at my house? Now he was making warning bells go off in my head.

"I think I'll just take the ticket."

The smile dropped from his face and his eyes went hard and cold. "Really? Such a shame."

He stood and I thought he was going back to his car to write the ticket. Instead, he yanked open my door and reached for me. He had popped my seatbelt and pulled me from the car before I could even process what was happening. I slapped at him.

"Let me go!"

"I don't think so. Pretty little whore like you? No, we're going to have us a bit of fun."

"I'm not a whore, you asshole!" I beat on him with a closed fist, but he didn't even seem to notice. I started kicking and thrashing, trying to break free. I lost my shoe in the struggle as he dragged me off the road and into the tree line.

"I saw you. At the club. You're a kinky little bitch, aren't you? Don't worry. I can give it to you better than the guy you were with."

"Officer Murray, let me go. I don't want this! It's assault!"

"Well now, it's just your word against mine. And I'm an upstanding citizen of this town, an officer of the law. You're just a woman making money off sex. Who do you think they'll believe?"

He started to tear at my shorts and abruptly stopped. I listened, trying to figure out what made him pause. A rustle came from a few feet away. My eyes went wide when I saw an alligator heading for us. I broke free of his slackened hold and bolted for my car. I didn't even bother to get my shoe. The moment my door closed, I glanced in my rearview mirror and saw Officer Murray running for his car. The gator snapped onto the hem of his pants and ripped the material before the man could get behind the wheel and shut the door. Thankfully, he didn't follow me. I floored it and didn't stop until I nearly busted through the gates of the compound.

Tears streaked my cheeks, and my hands shook. I swiped at my face, thankful I hadn't bothered with mascara. A guy knocked on the roof of my car, making me jump.

He bent down and his gaze softened when he got a look at me. "Damn, sweetheart. You okay?"

"R-Rooster. I need to see him."

"Shit. You're Alora, aren't you?"

I nodded and sniffled, wiping my tears from my cheeks. Didn't do any good. They kept falling. "Can I come through please? I don't feel safe out here."

He stood abruptly and opened the gate then waved me through. I pulled over to the nearest building, which I assumed was their clubhouse. I shut off the car and got out, the hot ground burning my shoeless foot. Someone lifted me into their arms, and I gave a slight shriek before grabbing hold. My vision blurred but I made out the word *President* on his cut.

"Come on, pretty girl. Let's get you inside and you tell me what's wrong," the man murmured.

"I want Rooster," I said.

"I know. I'm afraid he's not here. When he said

he didn't want to leave you, I hadn't realized he meant because you were in trouble."

Leave me? Is that why he hadn't come to see me? I didn't know how to feel about him leaving town and not saying a word, calling, or so much as texting the entire time. It made me feel like the cheap whore Officer Murray had called me.

"I wasn't until today," I said. "A police officer pulled me over for speeding. Said he'd let me off with a warning, but only if he got something in return. I told him no and the next thing I knew he was pulling me from the car. If an alligator hadn't come along, he would have... have..."

I swallowed hard, unable to even say the words. Things like that happened in the news and in movies. You never expected to be on the receiving end. Someone handed me a bottle of water, but I couldn't hold it. My hands shook so bad I almost dropped it.

"My name's Charming. I'm the President of the Devil's Boneyard. I sent Rooster out of town on a job. He didn't want to go, didn't want to leave you, but I didn't give him a choice. I'm sorry for that."

"Why hasn't he at least called?" I asked.

"Probably doesn't want you on anyone's radar." Charming took the seat across from me. "Do you know the name of the officer who tried to hurt you? He did only try, right?"

I nodded. "He wasn't able to get very far. Thanks to that gator. I think they're my new favorite animal."

He smiled. "I bet."

"It was Officer Murray."

Someone leaned down and whispered in Charming's ear. His jaw hardened and he glared at the older man. I saw the patches on his cut. *Scratch -- VP*. "Why the fuck am I just now finding out about this?

Let me guess, you told Cinder."

Scratch shrugged. "You said you were busy when I tried to talk to you."

"So Rooster knew something was off about Murray, and that he had Alora in his sights? No wonder the bastard didn't want to go." Charming sighed and closed his eyes a moment. "All right. I can admit, I fucked up. Note to self, pull my head out of my ass more often."

Scratch chuckled. "You said it, not me."

"All right, Alora. Here's what we're going to do. One, we're going to find your other shoe. After that, I'm going to have two men go with you to your place. Pack enough clothes and whatever else you need for at least a few days. You can stay at Rooster's house. I'll make sure he hauls ass back here immediately." Charming reached over and patted my hand. "We'll keep you safe."

"He saw us," I said. "Officer Murray. He saw Rooster and me. That's why he did it. Said I was a whore."

The two men shared a look. I could tell they didn't understand, and I wasn't sure I wanted to explain. I'd never been embarrassed before, but after dealing with Officer Murray I wasn't feeling overly confident.

Scratch knelt beside my chair. "Saw you? You mean he's been watching you in your house?"

I shook my head and my cheeks flushed. "I asked Rooster to take me to The Black Rose. I'd heard about it, but had never been. He got us a room. Officer Murray said he watched us. I feel so dirty now. He took something beautiful and ruined it."

Scratch and Charming held each other's gazes another moment, seeming to communicate silently with one another.

"I know guys like you can be possessive, and you're wondering why Rooster would have agreed to take me there. He said he wouldn't share me, but he'd give me that much if it's what I wanted. I got off on it at the time. If I'd known Officer Murray was there, I'd have never done it."

I twisted my hands in my lap. Rooster had wanted me all to himself. I'd known that and pushed anyway. After today, I never wanted to go back to The Black Rose ever again. And I sure the hell didn't want anyone watching me have sex. I felt like I needed to scrub myself under boiling hot water.

"Something of an exhibitionist, huh?" Charming asked.

I shrugged. I didn't really want to label myself as one thing or another. I liked sex, and I liked to experiment with different things. Even though I liked being tied up and spanked, enjoyed different sex toys, and liked a bit of pain with my pleasure, I wouldn't say I was part of the BDSM lifestyle. I was just... me. Or I had been until today.

Charming gripped my chin and forced me to look at him. "Nothing to be ashamed of, pretty girl. As long as both parties are willing, it's not wrong."

"Unless it's illegal," Scratch muttered.

Charming nodded. "Right. Except then."

I wasn't sure I wanted to ask what they meant by that. When would it be illegal?

"You're just going to let me into Rooster's house? What if he doesn't want me there?"

Scratch threw back his head and laughed. "Girl, you're a riot. Not want you there? Hell, I'm surprised that kid hasn't tossed you over his shoulder and carried you home. Everyone here knows he's ready to claim you."

"I'd told him I wanted to take things slow, but…" I placed a hand over my stomach.

Charming let out a low whistle. "So it's like that, huh? No fucking way he knew before he left or I'd have had a bigger fight on my hands."

The way he talked made it sound like Rooster would want this baby. Maybe he would. He'd said he wanted me to be his. Unless he didn't want children, I had to assume he planned to knock me up at some point. Looked like it just happened sooner rather than later.

"I only found out recently. I don't know how he'll react. I'd told him I was on birth control, and I was, but I'd forgotten the medication I'd taken almost two weeks before had made my pills pretty much useless. The doctor had mentioned it to me, and it slipped my mind." I looked from one man to the other. "I swear I didn't get pregnant on purpose."

"I'm going to send Havoc and Ashes with you," Charming said. "Havoc is my Sergeant-at-Arms, and he's one scary bastard. He's also got a woman and kids. Ashes also has a family. I didn't want you to feel uncomfortable with two single men going with you."

It was clear they thought today had damaged me. It had, but not quite in the way they believed. I wasn't scared of these men. If they were anything like the Devil's Fury, then I was safe here. Didn't matter if they were married or single. If they lived by the same code, then they'd never hurt a woman or child.

"Do you think Rooster has a place for my desktop? I could use my laptop, but I prefer my regular computer." Not to mention, I kept my laptop bare bones. If I wanted to work on any marketing or play with some older projects, I'd need the apps and files on my desktop.

Scratch stood and placed a hand on my shoulder. "Darlin', you bring whatever you want. If he doesn't have a place for it, we'll make one. You want to pack up your entire house? We'll see that it's done. You get what you need immediately and make a list of anything else you want. I'll personally see that it's handled."

"Thank you."

Charming leaned forward. "Just so you know. When Rooster gets home, he's not letting you move back to your house. If he wanted to claim you before, knowing you're carrying his kid is going to make him even more determined. He won't let you out of his sight."

"Great. Just what I wanted. An overbearing biker, breathing over my shoulder every second of the day. There better be orgasms and egg rolls involved, or I may murder him."

Scratch choked back a laugh. "I think I like this girl. You kill him, I'll help you hide the body."

"Fucking hell, Scratch! Don't encourage her! Next thing you know, we'll have another Jordan on our hands, and one of that woman is plenty." Charming stood. "I'll go call Havoc and Ashes, get them here soon as they're able. I'll leave her in your hands until then, although I'm starting to doubt that's such a good idea. It's like handing knives to toddlers."

Scratch flipped him off, but I could tell the two actually liked each other. Someone brought a plate to the table with a salad and piece of grilled fish. The guy blushed a bit as he set it down.

"I heard what you said, about being pregnant. Thought maybe you'd like something to eat."

"That was sweet of you."

"This is Hunter. He's one of our newest Prospects. Good kid. Great chef." Scratch slapped him on the back.

"Thanks, VP." He smiled and hurried off.

"Why don't we make a list of things you need right away," Scratch said. "I'll grab a pad and pen. With you being a bit... frazzled... you may forget something."

"Good idea." I smiled. "I appreciate everything y'all are doing for me."

"You're family, Alora. You and the little one inside you."

Family. It was a foreign concept. Sure, I'd had my mom, but it had been the two of us all my life. With her gone, I didn't have anyone except Gypsy. Although, while I'd been with the Devil's Fury, I'd met my cousin, Meredith. I hadn't even known about her, and she hadn't known about me. We'd kept in touch, but we didn't have a lot in common, other than our DNA. It made conversations a bit awkward.

"I'm not sure I know how to be part of a big family."

"For starters, you're going to let us handle Officer Dipshit. He won't be bothering you again, not when we're done with him." Scratch narrowed his eyes and I imagined he was thinking of ways to gut the cop. I wouldn't stand in the way. The asshole deserved whatever he got. If he'd tried that with me, there was no telling what else he'd done to other women.

"I'm not too eager to go into town on my own. Or even to my house. You didn't see the look in his eyes. He... changed." I sucked in a breath. "I have no problem with you sending someone with me. Give me as many bodyguards as you want."

Scratch tapped the edge of my plate. "Eat up.

We'll work on that list while we wait for the others. You don't have to be afraid, Alora. We won't let Officer Murray or anyone else hurt you. We protect our own."

I nodded and took a bite of the fish. I had to admit he was right. Hunter was an amazing chef. I wondered if he'd be willing to share recipes. Or better yet, just come to the house and cook for us. I wasn't a complete disaster in the kitchen, but I wasn't going to win any awards either. The dressing didn't taste like anything I'd had from the store and I wondered if he'd made it. The fish was nice and flaky, and seasoned to perfection.

Scratch helped me make a list of what I'd need, including all the things I'd have to take for Gypsy too. By the time we'd finished, and I'd eaten all the food on my plate, Havoc and Ashes had arrived at the clubhouse. It seemed Charming had already filled them in on everything. Because I was so rattled, Ashes offered to drive me in his truck, after assuring me he didn't care about Gypsy shedding all over his seats.

Another Prospect, Carlos, offered to drive my car to Rooster's house. I didn't plan on going anywhere if I didn't have to, but I didn't exactly want to leave it at the clubhouse either. I handed him my keys and got into the truck with Ashes.

On the way to my house, I saw my shoe lying in the road. Havoc stopped and got it for me, passing it through the window, before he took a few pictures of the grass and the marks where Officer Murray had dragged me off the road. I didn't see the alligator and wondered if it was still lurking nearby. Havoc didn't seem worried, even though he was on his motorcycle without any protection from a gator attack. My heart was racing when we pulled into my driveway. I took the list of items I needed and went into the house with

Havoc and Ashes on my heels.

"I'll stay down here," Havoc said. "Tell me what you need, and I'll start gathering it up. Ashes can go upstairs with you."

"Other than the things in my bedroom and bathroom, everything else on the list is downstairs." I handed it to him. "I can just double check the items before we leave."

"I'll start with the dog stuff."

"Call Shade before you dismantle her computer," Ashes said. "You break it, I'm not saving your ass when she has a meltdown."

Havoc snorted. "If I can live with Jordan, I think I'll be okay."

"True enough," Ashes muttered. "Only you think your psycho woman is cute. The rest of us have common sense and hide from her."

"I think I need to meet this Jordan," I said. "She sounds like fun."

"Oh, fuck me." Ashes sighed. "Rooster isn't going to be happy about this. Just keep away from Jordan until your man is back home. I'm not getting blamed for any bad habits you pick up."

I didn't know what to make of these two. I decided to ignore them and go pack my things. Thankfully, my trunk of toys wasn't see-through. I pulled it out from under the bed and Ashes carried it to the top of the stairs. I got my suitcase out of the closet and filled it with enough clothes to last me a week.

I made sure I had my favorite shirts. I grabbed the black one that said "I like coffee and maybe three people" even though in all honesty, until now, it had been coffee and maybe *one* person. Looked like I'd have to socialize more now that I would be part of the

Devil's Boneyard family. I also grabbed the purple shirt that said, "I could agree with you but then we'd both be wrong."

I heard a snicker behind me as I shoved the shirt into my bag. I eyed Ashes over my shoulder. "What?"

"You'll want one of those for every conversation you have with Rooster. That man will insist he's right, even after you've shown him proof he's wrong."

"So… he's like every other man on the planet?" I asked, smiling sweetly.

Ashes huffed at me and gave me a mock glare, but I saw the humor in his eyes. At least someone thought I was funny. I packed a few more shirts, including my favorite that said, "I'm not hard to please. Just do what I say."

I only grabbed two pair of shoes, other than the Converse I already had on. The bathroom stuff took longer, and I ended up piling it into a cardboard box.

It took about an hour to gather everything and load it into the back of Ashes' truck. Thankfully, Officer Murray didn't make an appearance. My neighbors kept to themselves, for which I was grateful. I wasn't sure I had the ability to deal with any more people for the day. I'd met my quota. Maybe I should have worn my "It's too people-y outside" shirt.

We pulled through the gates of the compound and Ashes took a left down the road. When he stopped in front of a two-story house, I thought he must have taken me to the wrong place. It was cute. Mint green with white trim. The windows didn't have shutters, but there were flowering bushes along the front of the house. It didn't look even a little like the type of home I thought a biker would have.

"This is Rooster's place?" I asked.

"Yep." Ashes got out of the truck. "He had a

smaller place until a month ago. Then he asked Charming for a home big enough for a family. Didn't take a rocket scientist to figure out why. He always intended for you to move in here with him."

I didn't even know what to do with that statement. Rooster's behavior wasn't rational. Who the hell got a bigger house for a family they didn't have with a woman they'd never met? I knew the bikers I'd met all lived by a different set of rules. I could understand it, somewhat. But this?

"You know that's certifiable right? He didn't even know me." I wasn't going to think about the fact he'd been following me weeks before I knew he existed. Stalking someone wasn't the same as getting to know them.

Ashes leaned against the side of the truck and looked at me through the window. "We tend to resist settling down for as long as possible. When the right woman comes along, that's it. We don't drag our feet."

"I wish I could be so certain of everything. Most days I feel like I'm just pretending to be an adult."

"Sweetheart, you have it figured out more than most. You're successful and have your shit together. Not many women your age can say the same." He smiled. "And men your age definitely can't claim the same. Most the ones I've known, myself included, were fuck-ups the first several decades of their lives."

I got out and went up to the porch. The white swing on the end beckoned to me. I walked over and sat down, putting it into motion. Ashes let Gypsy out and she raced around the yard before disappearing down the side of the house. I started to stand, but Havoc waved me off.

"She'll be fine. Can't escape the compound no matter how far she roams. We'll get a fence up this week." He hefted one of my bags and carried it to the front door, setting it inside the house. "Let her explore her new territory for now, and you should do the same. Figure out where you want your computer. I've asked Shade to come over and hook it up for you."

"Thank you. I feel like I've said that more in the last few hours than I have in months. I only hope Rooster doesn't freak out when he gets here and finds his house turned upside down."

"Nah. He'll love it."

The two of them unloaded everything. Ashes carried my bedroom and bathroom boxes to the master suite while I set up Gypsy's items in the kitchen and pantry. I checked his fridge and wrinkled my nose. It looked like he hadn't bothered to clean out the perishables before he'd left. I tossed out everything expired, then took stock of the cabinets and pantry.

"If you need groceries, do an online order and ask one of the Prospects to pick it up," Havoc said from behind me. "He'll bring everything to the house and carry it inside for you. Hell, if you tell him where you want it, he'll even put it all away."

"I think I can put my own groceries away, but I'll keep it in mind for when I'm too fat to stand up."

"Holy shit," Ashes said as he stopped next to Havoc. "You really are pregnant, aren't you? I mean, I heard the words, but I guess it didn't really register until now."

"Looks like our family is growing again," Havoc said.

Ashes groaned. "If she's pregnant, that means at least one other woman around here is. Doesn't this sort of thing always happen in pairs or flocks?"

"We're not chickens," I said.

"He's not wrong though," Havoc said. "Every

club we know, when one woman finds out she's pregnant, it's not long before another one is. I know it won't be my woman, so I'll leave that up to the rest of you. The three kids I have are more than enough."

"You have three kids?" I asked, trying to picture the giant with children. Charming had mentioned Havoc was a family man, but after meeting the guy, it was hard for me to imagine. He looked scary as hell. Then again, from what Ashes said, everyone thought his wife was psycho. I wasn't sure I wanted to meet those kids.

"Lanie is our daughter by blood," Havoc said. "But we've adopted two other children. A daughter, Salem, and a son, Taggart. They're good kids. Most of the time. Lanie is nine now. We adopted Salem when she was three, but she turned seven recently. Taggart is the oldest at fifteen. He was twelve when we brought him home."

"I only have two. Oliver is six and Drake is five. Someone will show you the family areas tomorrow. You'll probably want to settle in tonight." Ashes rapped his knuckles on the wall. "We'll get out of your hair, but if you need anything let us know."

"I don't know how to reach anyone," I admitted.

"Give me your phone." Havoc held out his hand. I gave it to him, and he tapped at the screen a few minutes and gave it back to me. "I put in my number, Ashes, Charming, Scratch, and Hunter. I'm sure Rooster will be back soon."

If they had family areas, how many others had children? If I did stay here with Rooster, at least our child would have friends. Maybe not any close in age, unless what they said was true and someone else was pregnant or would be soon.

I wondered how long it would take Rooster to

get here. It felt awkward being in his home without his knowledge. To keep my mind occupied, I started unpacking my things. I didn't dare pick up my computer, but I did scout out the rooms to find a spot for it. Rooster didn't have a computer desk set up anywhere, and I didn't want to put it in the kitchen, which meant I'd need my desk from home. Or at least a desk from somewhere.

Whoever Shade was, I hoped he wouldn't be put out when he got here and realized we couldn't set up the machine. I hated wasting anyone's time, especially since I knew how precious every minute was. I didn't think my editor would appreciate my latest distraction. Hopefully she didn't come after me with a pitchfork when I gave her the bad news that my writing had come to a halt again.

Chapter Eight

"Nymphomaniac: a woman as obsessed with sex as an average man."
   -- Mignon McLaughlin

Rooster

I stared at my phone, dread crawling down my spine. *Get home now!*

The Pres wouldn't send me something like that unless it was important. I didn't know what the hell was going on. Had something happened to Alora? Was the club under attack?

I looked around and wondered if I could slip out unnoticed. For Charming to pull me off this job, I knew it had to be something big. He'd stressed the importance of this mission and sent me on my way, despite the fact I'd fought to stay with Alora. I hadn't liked the way Officer Murray had watched her. I could only imagine what she thought of me right now. I couldn't risk calling her, not without getting her tangled up in this mess.

A dainty hand slid across my shoulder. The red tipped nails meant it had to be one person in particular. Simone. She wouldn't be happy when I disappeared. No fucking way I could give her a heads up. Too risky. I hated to bail on her, but Charming would probably send someone to replace me.

"You coming to my room tonight?" she asked, trailing her fingers down my chest. She knew to watch where she touched me. She'd found out the hard way.

"No." I gripped her wrist and pulled her hand off me. "Go find someone else tonight, Simone. I've got shit to do."

Like figure out how the fuck Demonic Reign had

popped back up on the map, and how I was going to get away from this hellhole without being too obvious. We'd gotten word about this chapter and Charming had volunteered the Devil's Boneyard to take out the trash. *Thanks for that, Pres.* Except, there were more men here than we'd realized. I didn't know if they only had this one chapter, or if there were others. This particular group of brothers were twenty strong. Too many for me to take on single-handedly.

Her eyes went hard and cold. "Fine. What-the-fuck-ever. It's not like you're all that anyway."

She stormed off and I heard a chuckle behind me.

"Pissed that one off pretty good." I cracked my neck and looked over my shoulder at Bruiser, their VP. "You got something better than little Simone?"

"Maybe. Saw a sweet piece in town earlier. Thought I'd hook up with her. See how she handles, if you know what I mean."

He slapped me on the back. "Bring her here and we'll party."

I nodded. "Gotta make sure I put her at ease first. You know how those bitches can be. Prissy on the outside, but a whore once you get them on their knees."

Bruiser laughed long and hard before walking off. The guy made my skin crawl. Hell, the entire fucking club did. At least I'd given them a plausible reason for me to head into town for a bit. Hopefully, no one followed me. I'd stashed my cut and anything else that might give me away in a storage locker at the bus depot. After I knew the coast was clear, I'd grab my shit and hit the road.

I finished my beer and lazily stretched, scanning the room. Most of the men were balls deep in pussy. I stood and headed outside, stopping at the edge of the parking lot to smoke a cigarette. I'd given up the habit years ago, but it gave me a good reason to be standing outside. No one came out after me. I waited another five minutes before getting on my bike and pulling away from their clubhouse.

I looped through town several times, but didn't see anyone following me. It only took me a moment to grab my shit. As disrespectful as it felt to ride without my colors on my back, I didn't dare put them on until I'd gotten further away from this place. I'd been on the road an hour before I pulled over and took my cut from my bag. I still didn't want to risk calling or texting anyone, so I got back on the road and didn't stop again until I needed gas.

I hadn't seen a single bike behind me, and only a few coming from the opposite direction. Thankfully, none of them had been from Demonic Reign. If Charming wanted to take them down, he'd have to find someone else to do it. I didn't think any one person could handle it. If it were up to me, I'd call in the other clubs and have each send a few men. The weeks I'd spent there, trying to gain their trust, I hadn't learned shit. Except about the evil crap they were into. Every last one of those fuckers were rapists, murderers, and they even had a few pedophiles in the mix. Seeing the women and kids they'd been abusing had been the hardest part of being there. Sitting back and doing nothing? It had been pure hell.

I wanted to drive straight through. I might have made it, but eight hours into my trip, exhaustion pulled at me. Stopping at a motel, I got a room so I could rest a bit and shower. I needed to get the Demonic Reign stench off me. If I thought calling in the law would do any good, I'd make an anonymous tip. Sadly, the locals were in the club's pocket. I could possibly get the Feds involved because of the kids. I'd hand over everything I had to Charming and let him make the call when I got home.

I stretched out on the motel bed and shut my eyes. Sleep pulled me under fast and hard. The only thing that woke me was the ringing of my phone. I blurrily stared at the screen and realized I'd only slept two hours. Since it was Charming, I knew I needed to answer.

"Yeah," I said, not bothering with pleasantries.

"You on your way home?"

"Yep. Just stopped to shut my eyes for a bit. I'll get back on the road soon."

"No, you need to leave now. You weren't the only plant in the club. Spider sent someone too. Word is the Demonic Reign are hunting you. Check your bike for any trackers, ditch anything you had in their clubhouse, and get the fuck out of there."

I jolted into action, getting off the bed and digging through my shit. Shade had given me a scanner before I'd left. I took it outside and went over the bike, looking for any bugs or trackers. It came back clean. If they were following me, then they'd hidden something in my other belongings.

I went through everything in my bag, and my clothes. It went off when I got to my boots. *What the fuck?* How the hell had they gotten something into my damn shoes? I pulled the right one off and looked along the sole. If I hadn't been looking, I'd have never caught it. There was a slight cut, and I found the tracker. Tiniest fucking thing I'd ever seen, which meant it was probably pricey as hell. I dropped it on the ground and crushed it, then grabbed my shit and left.

The thought of those men coming for me,

following me home, had shaken the tiredness from my mind and body. I drove as fast as I dared without calling too much attention to myself. By the time I pulled up to the gates of the compound, I was ready to drop. I hoped like hell Charming didn't want to go over anything today. I needed a shower and sleep. Lots of sleep. After that, I wanted to check on Alora.

The Prospect opened the gate and I pulled through. Heading straight to the house, I paused on the street out front when I saw Alora's car in the driveway. Why the hell was she here? Is that why Charming told me to come home? Had something happened to her? Why the fuck had he been so secretive?

I shut off the bike and went inside, noting the few changes to the house. Some of her things were spread around the living room. It seemed she'd made herself at home. I smiled, liking the idea of her settling in. Now if I could just find a way to keep her here. Permanently. I didn't think for a second she'd changed her mind and moved in voluntarily.

"Alora?" I called out.

I heard footsteps upstairs and took the steps two at a time. She rubbed her eyes as she came into the hallway. Her hair was mussed from sleep. The pajamas she had on were adorable. The shorts were pink with yellow sheep printed on them and the tank was the same shade as the sheep.

"Rooster?" she asked. "You're home!"

"I take it you're the reason Charming called me back early?"

She nodded and tears gathered in her eyes. I hurried closer and pulled her into my arms. "Alora, what's wrong? Did something happen?"

"We can talk about it later. You have to be tired.

Charming said it would take you a while to get back. Did you drive straight through?"

"Baby girl, there has to be a reason you're in my house. Not that I didn't love coming home to you, but… are you in trouble?"

"Let's talk about it tomorrow. Why don't I run a hot shower for you?"

I wanted to argue with her, make her talk, but I'd give her a little space. Whatever was going on, she was safe as long as she was in my house. I just had to make sure she didn't leave before I found out what was going on.

"All right, baby girl. Go start the shower. I'm sure I stink, and I'm covered in road dust."

She hurried off and I followed. The bedding was rumpled, clothes had been discarded on the floor, and there were bags near the bathroom door. I heard the shower starting and I stripped out of my boots and clothes. I padded into the bathroom and noticed Alora had removed her clothes. She stood under the spray and held out a hand. I went to her, shutting the shower door behind me.

"I think I like coming home when you're here waiting for me," I said.

She reached up and placed her hand on my cheek. "I wasn't sure how you'd feel about my stuff being everywhere. I only brought the essentials for now."

For. Now. It gave me hope she wanted this to be a more permanent thing. I honestly thought she'd keep fighting me. I wondered what had changed. I let her wash me, enjoying the feel of her hands on my body. As exhausted as I was, my cock barely twitched. Being balls deep inside her would feel like heaven, but I needed sleep first. I wouldn't take my pleasure without knowing I could give Alora multiple orgasms. Right now, I'd probably fall asleep in the middle of sex. Talk about humiliating.

I washed Alora and noticed the way her breath hitched when I slid my palm across her stomach. My gaze held her, and I saw pain, uncertainty, and so much more in the depths of her eyes. I pressed my hand against her more firmly and felt the tremor that ran through her body.

"What's going on, baby girl? Did someone hurt you?" I looked over the skin around my palm and under it. I didn't see any bruising.

"I didn't want to tell you this way, but if I don't tell you before you meet with Charming or the others, they could say something first." She took a breath and placed her hand over mine. "Killian, I'm... pregnant."

It felt like the earth shifted under my feet. "What?"

"I didn't do it on purpose! I'd forgotten some medication I'd taken had made my pills ineffective during the time we were together. I was coming here to tell you about the baby, even though I hadn't heard from you in weeks. Except I got pulled over by Officer Murray."

I wrapped my arms around her, holding her close. I could only imagine what Officer Dumbass had said to her. I seriously hated that prick.

"Killian, he... he was going to rape me."

Her words were whisper soft, but I heard them. Each one penetrated my skin like a bullet straight to the heart. Jesus. My woman had been attacked while I was off on a mission I hadn't even wanted in the first place. And she was pregnant? That fucker had dared touch her, hurt her, while she carried my child? I wanted his blood!

"He's dead, Alora. I will end him myself if I have to. No one hurts you, especially that way, and gets away with it." My club should have told me! Why the hell hadn't Charming said anything? He knew how I felt about Alora. They all did. It felt like a betrayal.

"Just hold me, Killian. I was worried you'd be angry. Think I tricked you. If I'd been paying more attention, I wouldn't have been speeding and maybe he'd have left me alone."

I shook my head. "No, baby girl. He wouldn't have. He was there, at The Black Rose. He watched you. Us. I saw the lust in his eyes and knew he'd be a problem. I should have told you."

"It's no one's fault, Killian. We can't hold ourselves responsible for his actions. He chose to drag me off the road. The evil inside him made him try to hurt me that way."

"Doesn't change the way I feel. I should have been here to protect you." I kissed her soft and slow. She meant so much to me. It didn't matter how long we'd been together. I'd known before we'd even spoken that she was meant to be mine.

I didn't like the fact Officer Murray was after her, but what he'd planned to do would have paled in comparison to what Demonic Reign would do to her. Being with me put her in the crosshairs of too many bad people. I knew there were plenty of families in the club now. Didn't change the fact I'd worry for her every time she left the compound. Putting her on lockdown wouldn't go over well.

"You should have been safe. If I'd claimed you, made you my old lady, the club would have been watching you better. I'm pissed as fuck those assholes didn't have anyone guarding you. Not only had Badger asked us to keep an eye on you, but they knew damn well I wanted you. I told Scratch I didn't trust that fucking prick, Murray."

"We can't change what's already happened, Killian. All we can do is move forward. I'm still not thrilled with the idea of being property."

I ran my hand up and down her back. "Then how about my wife? Would you be okay with that title?"

She peered up at me. "Seriously? You want to marry me? It's because of the baby. Look, women have babies on their own all the time. You don't have to do something like that just because I'm pregnant."

"Alora?"

"What?" she asked.

"Shut up." I smiled. "I don't want to marry you because you're carrying my kid. I'd have married you the day you opened the door and got all snarky with me. I thought you were cute as fuck. Like a prickly hedgehog."

"Word of advice, Killian. Don't compare your fiancée to a rodent."

"Technically, they aren't rodents. They're mammals. And cute. Like you."

She sighed and pressed her forehead against my chest. "We're going to fight a lot, aren't we?"

She considered this a fight? Well, shit. We were going to have a long, hard road if that was the case. Far as I was concerned, this was more like... foreplay. I liked bantering with her. Loved her sassy comebacks, the fire in her eyes, and the flush to her cheeks when she went off on me. Just made me want to kiss her senseless, then fuck her until she was all sated and smiling again.

"We'll have to agree to disagree. I don't consider this a fight."

She snorted. "Of course you don't. So, head to the courthouse? I guess we need a license and... whatever else is required in this state to get married. Do they do blood tests here?"

"Don't need any of that, unless you just want to stand up in front of the judge."

"Killian, I don't pretend to know everything in the world, but I do know you need an officiant of some sort to get married. Judge, priest, whatever."

I smiled. "Or a hacker. Shade can have the documents on file with the courthouse in no time. You want to be married without all the fuss? Just say the word. I'll get him started on it when we get out of the shower."

"You're serious?" she asked, brow furrowed. Even her nose wrinkled in the most adorable way.

"Yep. Won't be the first time someone around here got hitched that way. In case you missed it, we aren't so great at following the rules. Unless they're *our* rules."

"Yeah, I kinda figured that part out already." She sighed and chewed on her bottom lip as she stared up at me. "All right. Let's do it. Get Shade to do... whatever it is he does. But I want a ring! If I'm off the market, I want everyone to know. For that matter, you better wear one too. I see some woman with her hands all over you and I won't be held responsible for my actions."

"Aww. Now you have me all excited about watching you put some club whore in her place. Remind me to take you to a party at the clubhouse sometime soon."

She rolled her eyes. "Naturally you think that's hot. You're not right in the head, Killian. Not even a little."

Couldn't exactly argue with her on that one. Instead, I kissed her. Wasn't every day I got married. Too bad I was too fucking tired to enjoy my wedding night. I'd have to make it up to her after I got some sleep. And I needed to find out what the hell was being done about Officer Murray. If she'd told them about the attempted rape, I knew the club was most likely already taking care of it.

I hoped the fucker paid in blood.

Chapter Nine
"Good girls go to heaven and bad girls go everywhere."
-- Helen Gurley Brown

Alora

"You know, when I said I wanted a wedding ring, this wasn't what I had in mind." I eyed the ring on my finger. It was beautiful. Stunning, even. It was also heavy as shit and I kept catching it on things. Nothing major. Just clothes, grocery bags, my hair. But hey, if anyone ever needed a DNA sample, they could just pull the hair strands from my ring.

"Alora, it took me a week to find that exact ring. Besides, I thought it was rather perfect for you." He took my hand and kissed the back of it.

He wasn't wrong. It was rather perfect for a romance writer. He'd found a ring made of diamonds in a platinum band, shaped like a rose. It was from some fairytale collection, and after I'd snooped online, I also knew it cost a fucking fortune. I hadn't needed something so flashy. A plain band would have been sufficient. Secretly, I adored the damn thing, and the man who'd given it to me was pretty spectacular too.

"You're right. It's perfect and I love it." I kissed his cheek. "But just remember you picked out this giant rock when we're playing and the damn thing nearly cuts your ball sac open."

He winced and paled a little, eyeing my ring like it had suddenly turned into a viper.

"Why are you taking me to the clubhouse in the middle of the day?" I asked, changing the subject. I'd found it odd he'd gotten a call and we suddenly needed to leave. What the hell was so urgent?

"Pres said to get our asses there. I'm just following orders, baby girl."

Yeah, yeah. I'd heard that often enough since he'd come home from wherever he'd been. He wouldn't talk about it. I'd asked and gotten some lame "club business" answer. If he thought he could go off and do something dangerous, and give me that stupid answer, he was going to learn quick that shit wouldn't fly. Even though he hadn't said a damn word about what happened, I'd seen how exhausted he was. He'd claimed it was from riding straight home, but I knew better. The shadows under his eyes had been building for weeks. Whatever he'd been doing, it had weighed heavy on him. I only wished he'd share some of the burden with me. Two sets of shoulders would make the load a bit lighter.

He helped me from the truck and held onto my hand as we walked into the clubhouse. I didn't see many people in the main area. Sam stood behind the bar, two barely dressed women were at a table in the corner, and that was it. I didn't think it was normal for it to be this empty. Rooster led me through to the back and pushed open a set of double doors with the Devil's Boneyard colors burned into the wood.

Every member I'd met, and it seemed there were still quite a few I hadn't, were seated around a large table. Rooster took a seat and pulled me down onto his lap. It didn't escape my notice I was the only woman in the room.

"I asked Rooster to bring his wife because this concerns her." Charming leaned back in his chair. "As you've been made aware, Officer Murray pulled her from her vehicle and tried to rape her. We don't tolerate that shit around here, especially when it happens to one of our women. Rooster may not have married her at that point, but she was already pregnant with his kid."

"So that's why we finally took action against the asshole?" Irish asked. "I've told you for years he was a problem. You didn't think he was all that bad. Looks like I needed this sort of proof to get your attention."

Charming held up a hand. "I didn't want to rock the boat with the local law unless it was necessary. I've already had a chat with the police chief. He's gotten a list of complaints against Murray that spans the last five years, but there wasn't ever any proof. The asshole was careful not to be caught in public or on camera pulling any of his shit. The chief was happy to let us handle it however we saw fit."

"So what did the club do?" Rooster asked. "Because this is the first time I've heard what's going on. I knew about the incident with Alora, but you've brushed me off every time I've mentioned making the dickhead pay."

"You know the shed at the back of the property?" Charming asked.

"He's there?" Rooster asked.

Charming nodded. "I haven't done much to him yet. I thought I'd give you a chance. First, I need to know if Alora is like Jordan or more like Clarity."

Rooster tensed. "What the fuck does that mean?"

Scratch huffed. "Relax, kid. He only wants to know if Alora wants to take a whack at him before we finish him off. Or is she more like my sweet woman and would prefer to stay home and let us handle it."

Wait. What? I looked at the men around the table, finding every single one staring at me. Except Rooster, who was too busy trying to see if he had developed laser vision. At least, I assumed that's why he was glaring at the innocent, defenseless table like he wanted to murder it. A quick glance proved there weren't scorch marks, so it seemed he hadn't developed a superpower.

"I don't think I understand," I said.

"Honey, he hurt you. Scared the shit out of you. Hell, you arrived here without one of your shoes and had a damn gator come out of the tall grass while the fucker had you pinned. I want to know if you want to take a pound of flesh and get justice for yourself, or do you want the club to take care of it?" Charming asked.

"You mean like... kill him?" I asked.

"You aren't the first woman he's pulled that shit with," Renegade said. "The others weren't so lucky. No gators came to their rescue. He's a dirty cop and needs to go down. Even if he went to prison, do you think he'd survive long inside? Because he wouldn't. As much fun as it might be to watch him get beaten, raped, and treated like a toilet for however long he managed to keep breathing while locked up, I think it's best we just make him disappear."

Wow. Okay. So they were really just going to kill a police officer. Apparently with the blessing of the police chief? Where the hell had I moved? The wild west? I didn't think stuff like this really happened. Wasn't it just fiction?

I searched myself, trying to decide if I had it in me to hurt someone. Take their life. Make them bleed. Then I thought about how I'd felt that day. I'd known what he planned, and I'd been unable to break free. Not until the gator came along. I really should go set some chickens loose in that area in hopes he catches a few as a snack. He deserved some sort of prize for what he'd done, even if he'd just been acting off animal instinct.

"I want to see him," I said. "I don't know if I

have it in me to do anything. I may decide I want to go home."

"You don't have to do this," Rooster said. "I can take care of him, Alora."

I placed my hand over his. "I know you can. I have complete faith in your ability to avenge me, but I need to know if I can handle this. Not necessarily me taking his life. More... can I handle this sort of life? Where you go off and people may die, or I could be put in danger because of the things you do. I need to know I can deal with whatever comes our way."

"All right. I don't like it. I get it though." He pressed a kiss to my cheek.

"You two head over to the shed. I'll let Havoc come with you. One way or another, that asshole will breathe his last before he disappears for good." Charming smacked his hand on the table. "Go on, you three. Get out of here."

I stood and Rooster took my hand as we walked back out to his truck. We followed Havoc through the compound. I saw the shed in the distance, thinking it seemed awfully small. I figured that was probably the point. Who would see something so benign and think a man was about to die there? It looked like a place to store garden tools. Assuming anyone in this place actually *used* garden tools. Then again, they might... even if it was for planting bodies instead of greenery.

We stood outside the closed doors and Havoc unlocked it, then slid the doors open. I took a breath before going inside. Someone had run electricity to the building, and a dim bulb cast a yellow-ish light into the space. Officer Murray had been stripped down, bound to a chair in the middle of the floor, and gagged. A jagged cut over his brow bled freely, and he had bruises covering every inch of him. Blood had soaked the ground under him, even though I didn't see more injuries. Until I noticed it was dripping from behind the chair.

I walked around him, his gaze locked on me in pure hatred. I winced and felt a little nauseated when I saw they'd ripped out his fingernails and severed his pinky and ring finger on one hand. I fought back bile, thinking maybe I should have gone home after all. I circled back to the front of him and studied the man who'd tried to do something so vile to me.

He didn't look so scary now. I also knew if he could get free, he'd have been long gone. The way they'd shackled him guaranteed he wasn't leaving unless they allowed it. I didn't think that was happening until his heart stopped beating. I wanted to say I was horrified. I should have been. Knowing he'd hurt other women, that he'd have hurt me… it changed things. Made me see the world a little different. I'd heard how contemptable my uncles were, but hearing something and experiencing it were two different things. I saw the news, watched the horrific things people did to each other every day. None of it really hit home since it hadn't happened to me. But this… this was different.

"How does it feel to be helpless? To be held against your will?" I asked.

He didn't make a sound. Just glared at me.

"You probably think this is all my fault. It's not. It's *your* fault. You're a sick, twisted man, Officer Murray. I've heard about the other women. The ones who weren't so lucky. You're a rapist. Men like you shouldn't wear a badge. You shouldn't be allowed to roam the earth, free to hurt whomever you want."

Rooster placed his hand on my shoulder. I knew he wanted me to leave. He didn't like me seeing this, being a part of it. The truth was I'd been pulled into this the moment Officer Murray dragged me from my car. The difference was that I got to finish it.

"The women he hurt..." I looked at Havoc. "What did he do to them?"

"Alora, sweetheart, you don't need to hear that shit," Rooster murmured.

"I can handle it," I said, hoping I sounded braver than I felt.

"Held them down or tied them up," Havoc said. "Raped them. In multiple ways."

Multiple... oh. I narrowed my eyes at the man. No, not a man. He was a monster. The world would be a better place without him in it, and every other person just like him. Those who preyed on the weak, the ones who got off on hurting people. Maybe there wasn't a way to cleanse the entire world, but knowing one less rapist was out there would help me sleep better at night.

Anger burned inside me. The pain and suffering he'd put those women through made me want to cry. I'd almost been one of them. I turned to Havoc, knowing he'd be the more logical. Rooster couldn't be reasoned with when it came to someone hurting me.

"I want him to pay, Havoc. Not only with his life, although I want that too. But first I have a favor."

"Name it," the Sergeant-at-Arms said.

"I want him to hurt the way he hurt those women. I know none of you are that sort of monster, even though I'm sure there's a bit of devil inside each of you. Find someone, or several someones, who will handle it. Make him cry. Make him beg. When he's close to dead from the abuse he's suffered, lock him up until he starves to death."

Havoc whistled. "Damn. You really might give

my woman a run for her money. I knew I liked you."

"Alora, are you sure?" Rooster asked.

I glanced at Officer Murray and saw his hate had turned to fear. Good. That's exactly what I wanted. He needed to be as scared as his victims. I knew it was wrong, and would likely stain my soul, but I felt those women deserved to be avenged like this.

"I'm positive."

Rooster wrapped his arm around me, holding on tight. Havoc approached the monster chained to the chair. "Looks like you get to keep breathing for now. Hope you're ready for some fun. That's what you told your victims, right? That you just wanted to play? That it would be *fun*?"

"I'm taking Alora home," Rooster said. "If y'all need me, you know where to find me."

Havoc nodded. "I'll make the arrangements for our friend here. I know exactly where to send him. Little whorehouse few hours from here. Some of the workers are there willingly. This dickwad won't be the first to be sent there to rot though. Don't worry. The men who frequent the place will make sure he wants to die."

I wasn't sure I liked the fact he knew about a place like that and hadn't tried to shut it down. But if some of the workers were willing, who was I to judge? It was the non-consensual ones I worried about. I hoped every last one was like Officer Murray and deserved being tortured.

Rooster led me outside and drove home in silence. When we pulled up to the house, Scratch was waiting for us with his woman, Clarity, and their two boys, Caleb and Noah. I got out and welcomed Clarity and the kids into the house, taking them to the kitchen for drinks and a slice of the pie I'd made earlier.

"You seem to be holding up well," Clarity said.

I eyed the boys, careful of how I worded things. "Havoc is seeing to my request."

She nodded. "I heard. I also heard something else, but Scratch made me promise to keep my mouth shut. I know what it's like to wonder if your man is safe. I can't tell you club business, except this one thing. The matter Rooster was sent to handle is being dealt with by multiple clubs. You should be safe and so is he. Charming is trying to keep it far from our doorstep."

Well, her explanation was vague as hell. It was likely also the best I'd get. Unless Rooster cracked and told me something. I thought monkeys might fly before that happened, and if books were going to become reality, I could think of better worlds to be stuck in than the *Wizard of Oz*. Evil witches, flying monkeys, and trees that threw apples at you? Hard pass.

I noticed the boys eyeing Gypsy and opened the back door. She raced outside and I handed the kids her favorite ball. "She loves to play fetch."

They waited for Clarity to give her permission. The second she nodded, they took off, running almost as fast as the dog. Maybe the three of them would wear each other out.

"You know, we might need to borrow Gypsy once a week," Clarity said, watching the kids squeal and chase the dog as she played keep-away with the ball.

"If you use my dog to make your kids sleep, I'm calling in babysitting favors when my little one gets here and keeps me up all night."

Clarity smiled. "I can handle that. I love babies."

I nodded. I always had too. "In theory, they're awesome. I like the way they smell, when they haven't pooped themselves. They're soft, sweet, and so innocent. I also haven't had to keep one twenty-four-seven hours a day, every day of my life. They've always gone back to their parents when they got fussy. I'm not sure I'm equipped to handle a newborn."

Clarity laughed. "You'll do fine. You handle Rooster like a pro, and he can be pretty childish."

"Rooster? Have you *met* your husband?"

"He's usually very serious. He's lightened up a lot since Noah was born. I've seen him laughing and joking more than I had until then. Did you know he has a daughter? Knocked up a club whore."

My jaw dropped. "What?"

She nodded. "Happened long before he met me. In fact, his daughter is older than me. Her name is Darian and she's married to Bull with the Dixie Reapers. She grilled me when she first found out. Hell, she damn near scared me. Scratch took up for me. He's so wonderful and I know I'm damn lucky to have him in my life."

"That's just… wow. I take it the two of you get along now?" I asked.

"Oh yeah. Darian is great with the kids. We don't get to see them too often, but we travel there once a year, and she usually comes to visit for Christmas and sometimes over the summer. Could be worse. If they were part of a club further out, it could be years between visits. I know Scratch feels bad about missing out on most of her life. Her mom hid her from him."

I couldn't imagine doing something so awful. Even when I'd thought Rooster might not want our baby, I'd known I had to tell him. I'd have walked if he didn't want to be a father, but I knew it was right to let him decide.

"Have you met all the old ladies yet?" Clarity

asked.

"No. Just you. I've heard about Jordan quite a bit, but we haven't had a chance to meet. How many others are there?"

"Let's see… There's Josie. She belongs to Jackal, although I sometimes it's more like he belongs to her. Janessa is with Irish. You have *got* to hear their story. It's crazy. Meg is with Cinder. He was the President before he decided to step down and Charming took over. Then there's Darby. She's such a sweetheart. She's Renegade's old lady. And Renegade's sister, Nikki, is with Ashes. And now there's you!" Clarity smiled. "There's not a ton of us, but when I got here, Josie was the only old lady. No one else had settled down yet."

What she called "not a ton" seemed like a lot to me. I hadn't made friends since I'd moved to town. It would be nice to meet everyone and see if we had anything in common, other than our men being part of the same club. I didn't know where I fit in with these people. What could I contribute? There probably wasn't a big need for writers.

"I'll plan a small gathering. Just the ladies and kids." Clarity reached over and patted my arm. "Everyone is going to love you. But please don't let Jordan scare you off. She can be a bit much to handle."

The more I heard about Jordan, the more intrigued I became. Who was she? She sounded like a badass woman who took charge. Maybe I could use her in a book.

Chapter Ten

"I promise to always be by your side. Or under you. Or on top."
-- Unknown

Rooster

I woke to the sound of my phone going off. My eyes felt like sandpaper as I opened them and scanned the dark room. I leaned over the side of the bed and saw my phone light up on the floor as it continued to ring. Alora groaned next to me and rolled over.

"Make it stop!" She grabbed her pillow and pulled it over her head. If only I could do the same.

Before I could answer the call, it abruptly stopped ringing. A text came through a moment later. I kept blinking my eyes, trying to focus on the screen. I was getting too damn old to stay up all night fucking my woman.

I rubbed my eyes and the words finally cleared enough for me to read the message. *Murray is dead. Hung himself.*

Well, shit. It wasn't the ending any of us had hoped for. The dead part was good, but I'd wanted him to suffer longer. I know Alora had as well. For someone who wrote happy endings, she sure did have a bloodthirsty streak. It had surprised the shit out of me when she'd sentenced Murray to his fate. Since she didn't seem to be having nightmares, and I hadn't noticed her behavior changing, I didn't think it was weighing on her.

"What's going on?" she asked, rolling back over to face me.

"Murray hung himself. He won't be hurting anyone ever again."

She flung her arm over her eyes and heaved a sigh. "Great. Wish it had been more painful for him. Guess the end result is the same."

"I don't think your readers will appreciate you putting him in your books. They tend to be on the fluffy, humorous side. Blood and guts may send them running."

She giggled and curled into me. "Very true. You'll just have to make sure I'm inspired when I need to write again. I'm taking a week off, though. My book is with my editor, and other than some marketing prep, I'm done until I start the next one."

"And what does a romance writer do when she has time off?" I asked.

She smiled and climbed on top of me, pressing her pussy against my cock. "I can think of plenty of things we can do, and they all have a happy ending. Unless you have to work."

Technically, I should. Demonic Reign was still out there. After a discussion with Charming, the club had decided anyone who had a woman wouldn't be helping with this one. We had too much to lose. Instead, he'd sent Gator, Magnus, and Shadow. I knew several other clubs were sending men, including the Mayhem Riders and Savage Knights. At the moment, it was mostly a recon mission. We needed to know if the chapter I'd tried to infiltrate was the only one, or if they still had brothers across the US.

"Anything I need to do will be local for right now. Besides, I don't want to be too far away from you. Clarity insists this is our honeymoon phase and the club shouldn't ask me to leave you for long."

"I like Clarity. I think I owe her some cake."

She wiggled, her slick pussy sliding along my cock. It went from semi-hard to fully erect in a matter of seconds. There was nothing sexier than watching my woman get turned on. Her eyes went dark, and she arched her back, thrusting her breasts up.

"Ride me. Make yourself come."

She lifted her hips, and I positioned my cock so she could slide down. I hissed in a breath at how hot and wet she was. Fucking perfection! She gripped me just tight enough to send pleasure rippling through me. Alora moved slow at first, teasing the both of us. I reached between us and rubbed her clit in small circles, keeping my touch light and slowly getting firmer.

She moaned and closed her eyes, her hips jerking a little. "God, Killian. You feel amazing."

"Come on my cock, beautiful. Get yourself off then I'll give you what you really want."

Her gaze locked onto mine as she rode me harder. When she came, she threw her head back and cried out my name. Her hips kept rocking against me until the last tremor faded. I flipped us, pinning her to the mattress and reached for the restraints I'd left attached to the bed. I bound her wrists before getting the other items I needed.

I warmed the lube in my hand before slicking her ass with it. I took my time, working first one finger then a second inside her. Alora whimpered and squirmed. I knew she wanted more, but she was at my mercy right now, which meant we were doing things my way. I picked up the vibrating anal plug and turned it on before easing it inside her.

She gasped, her eyes wide. "Oh, God. Killian! It's…"

"Big," I finished for her. Yeah, it was. We hadn't used this one yet, even though she'd picked it out online last week. I hadn't told her it had arrived this morning. I'd been saving it for the right moment.

Her eyes nearly rolled back in her head when I turned up the vibrations. I gripped her ankle and secured it at the corner of the bed, then did the same to the other, leaving her spread wide. Her pussy lips parted, giving me a sexy, tempting view. I knew when I slid inside her, the combination of the anal plug and my cock would make her feel incredibly full. Hell, I'd be able to feel the vibration of that thing all along my dick. I'd be lucky if I didn't blow within seconds.

"Ready for me, baby girl?" I asked.

"Yes! Please... Make me come, Killian. Fill me up."

I braced myself over her and ran my cock along her slit before pushing inside. I clenched my jaw, feeling the plug through the thin tissue separating my dick from the toy. Jesus fuck! I wasn't going to last. No damn way. I didn't hold back. Couldn't.

I rocked against my woman, slamming my cock into her. I adjusted my angle so my pelvic bone rubbed her clit with every stroke. She tensed and strained, yanking at the Velcro cuffs on her wrists and ankles. The second I felt the warmth of her release, I let go. I thrust through my orgasm, wanting to drag it out as long as possible. I came so fucking hard it felt like I'd been turned inside out.

I kissed Alora, wondering how I'd ever gotten so lucky to find someone like her. She blew my fucking mind every damn day, and not just in the bedroom. She amazed me. The way she'd handled seeing Murray in the shed, the incredible desserts she made, and her funny, erotic books... all of it, and so much more. Every single thing about her pulled me in, made me want to just hold her, fuck her, and brand myself on her. She was mine, and I wanted the world to know it.

"You good?" I asked.

She nodded, breathing heavy. "Yeah, but…"

"But what?"

"I want to come again."

I fought back my laughter. The woman was insatiable. I'd made her come seven times in a row the other night, before I'd even got my dick anywhere near her. Using my hands and toys, I'd made her soak the bed, and still she'd wanted more. Greedy little wench.

I reached into the bedside table drawer and pulled out the small vibrator I kept for when I wanted to tease her awake. I twisted it until it turned on, then placed the small toy against her clit. It nestled perfectly between the lips of her pussy, and with our bodies still joined, it was easy for me to keep it in place without using my hands. My cock twitched and I felt another bit of cum spurt into her. No way I could go again, but it seemed I hadn't completely drained my balls like I'd thought.

I was still hard enough I could use slow, shallow thrusts to heighten her pleasure. Although, the vibrations along my dick were almost too much for me to handle. I was sensitive as fuck right now. I managed to get her off three more times before I pulled out, watching as my cum slid from her body. It was a sight I'd never tire of seeing.

"You all wrung out now?" I asked.

She shook her head. "I don't know why I'm so… so…"

"Horny?" I asked, smiling down at her.

"Yeah. It's like I can't come enough times. I just want more and more orgasms. Worse than usual."

I had a feeling it might be part of her pregnancy. I seemed to recall Havoc saying something about Jordan wanting sex all day every day when she was pregnant. Well, when she wasn't threatening to rip off his balls, or anyone else's. Of course, we tried not to bring those days up. She'd lost the baby and been devastated. I hoped like hell Alora didn't have that problem.

I grabbed the trunk of toys and spent the next hour making Alora scream my name. It wasn't until she literally passed out from coming so hard that I was able to put everything away and released her from the restraints. I curled around her, holding her against my body. I breathed in her scent and knew I'd found my home. It wasn't a building or a place. It was her. As long as I was with Alora, it didn't matter where we were or who we were with. I'd always be home when I was with her.

"Love you," I murmured, knowing she wouldn't hear me. I wasn't ready to say the words when she was awake. She'd start going off again about how we hadn't known one another long enough. For someone who wrote sappy shit, she sure didn't believe in love at first sight.

"Love you too," she whispered.

Fuck. I tightened my hold on her. "You awake?"

She nodded. "It's crazy, right? To feel so intensely about each other so fast? Real life doesn't work like that."

"Says who?" I asked. "Because society thinks you should date someone for a certain amount of time, it makes it wrong when you have an instant connection? I call bullshit. I think those people are jealous. I don't give a fuck what anyone thinks, Alora. You're mine and I love you. Simple as that."

"I didn't think I wanted this. To settle down. There were things I wanted to do, places to see, fun to be had. I didn't realize what I'd be missing out on by pushing you away. If you hadn't been an obstinate

Harley Wylde   Rooster/Cuffs & Kink Duet

mule, we wouldn't be together right now."

"Did you just call me an ass?"

"I didn't use the word ass. I said mule. But yeah, same difference." She snickered. "If anyone asks, you can always say it's a pet name because your dick is huge."

"Baby girl, that saying is 'hung like a horse.' No mention of mules or asses."

"I'm a writer. I can make shit up if I want to. It's my superpower."

"Go to sleep, crazy girl. Otherwise I may be tempted to put my mule-sized dick somewhere."

She wiggled her ass against me. "I'd be okay with that."

"Why am I not surprised? Sleep! Christ, you're like the sexy version of the Energizer Bunny."

"My name's Alora not Jessica."

I blinked and tried to process that. "What the fuck does that mean?"

"You know… Jessica Rabbit? The sexy redhead from *Who Framed Roger Rabbit*?" She looked at me over her shoulder. "Get it? Energizer Bunny. Sexy rabbit. See what I did there?"

I closed my eyes and tried not to groan at her adorable, quirky, corny self. "Sleep! Now. Close your eyes and don't say another word. Some of us are old and need to rest."

She wiggled against me again and fuck if I wasn't already half-hard.

"Your mouth says you're old. Your dick says 'Yee Haw, Motherfucker.'"

I couldn't do it. I tried. I really did. At first, I shook in silence but then the laughter came out. It didn't escape so much as erupt from me. I laughed until I damn near cried. This woman! The crazy ass shit she said and did would keep me amused for an eternity and then some.

"Don't ever change, Alora. You are one in a million, and you're all mine."

"Mm-hm. All of me. Including my pussy. Feel free to show it who's boss anytime you want. Lick it, pound it, come inside it."

"Woman, do you ever shut up? Or think of anything other than sex?"

She was quiet a few minutes and I thought she'd fallen asleep. "No, I'm pretty sure I'm always thinking about sex. Especially since experiencing the wonder that's your mule-sized dick. Can't get enough of it."

"I hadn't noticed," I said dryly. At this rate, I'd be getting her off with toys more often than my cock or I'd wear out my poor dick and balls. I could see it now. In twenty years, I'd be popping blue pills just to keep up with her.

She yawned so wide her jaw cracked. "Night, Killian."

Before I could respond, a soft snore came from her. I shook my head and closed my eyes. Never a dull moment. Not with Alora.

Luckiest bastard on earth! Because she's mine.

Chapter Eleven
"Morning Sex. Proven to be more effective than coffee..."
-- Unknown

Alora
One Month Later

Everything had been quiet. A little too much so. With Officer Murray out of the way, I felt safe when I was in town. The first few times, Rooster had gone with me or had me followed. I couldn't blame him. He had a protective streak a mile wide. No, more like ten miles wide. The man could be suffocating at times.

He'd insisted on going with me to the doctor to confirm my pregnancy, even though I'd already done that. It apparently didn't count if he wasn't with me. Between the date of my last period and the times Rooster and I had had sex, Dr. Chansy estimated I was two months along. Thankfully, I hadn't experienced morning sickness. The only side effect I seemed to have gotten was an increased sex drive. Poor Rooster. I'd lost count of how many times he'd walked in the door only to have me pounce immediately, unzip his pants, and climb him like a tree.

Of course, he always came so I didn't think it was a hardship for him. I nearly snickered to myself. *Hard.* Yeah, being pregnant had reduced my humor to that of a twelve-year-old boy. I was glad I hadn't said anything inappropriate in front of the kids yet, but it was bound to happen sooner or later.

I'd met Clarity, Josie, and Janessa at the pavilion for a bit of girl time. Although, I kind of thought they just wanted to get their hands on my latest book. Once they'd found out who I was, they'd been hounding me for reading material. It was nice though. We got together at least twice a week just to hang out. I hadn't really had this sort of relationship before. They'd read my work, then we'd discuss it. Sometimes their questions would spark an idea for another book or a spinoff series. I had a notebook full of scribbles and little tidbits I'd gleaned from these meetings. At this rate, I would never write them all. I'd be dead before I had the chance because I probably had enough notes to write a book a month for the next two hundred years.

I watched Allegra and Caleb across the grassy field. The littles were closer, playing on the slide and swings. The ones who felt too big for such childish things, but secretly yearned to go play, had overtaken another table and were playing on their phones and tablets. But the two older ones had held my attention the last ten minutes.

"Why are you staring at them?" Janessa asked softly.

"I'm waiting on him to find his courage," I said.

"Wait, what do you mean?" Josie asked, twisting to look at the kids.

Before I could respond, Caleb darted forward and pressed his lips to Allegra's, only to pull back almost immediately. They both looked like startled deer as they stared at one another and I couldn't help but smile. Those two were adorable.

"Oh, shit," Josie muttered. "Jackal is going to be pissed."

Clarity glared at Josie. "Why? My boy not good enough?"

Josie held up a hand. "Trust me. When it comes to Jackal and his precious angel, *no one* is good enough. A saint could walk through the door and profess his undying love for her, and Jackal would probably crucify him, then put him on display in the yard as a warning to anyone else who dared think they could kiss his daughter."

I was still watching the kids. Allegra had gotten over the shock first. She'd given Caleb a shy smile then reached over to take his hand. Now their heads were bent close as they talked.

"I won't tell if you don't," I said. "But I think it's cute as hell. Besides, those two would be good together, don't you think?"

"Caleb does have a lot of patience," Clarity said.

"Allegra had some delays when she was smaller. Mostly that she couldn't speak," Josie said, focusing on me. "She's improved so much, and she's incredibly smart. But a lot of kids at school give her a hard time, remembering how she was when she was little. Caleb is her champion. He won't let anyone give her shit."

"And that would be why I spend so much time in the principal's office," Clarity said. "Not because my boy is a troublemaker, but because he insists on defending Allegra every time someone bullies her. I should have seen this coming. I'm not worried about Scratch's reaction, but Josie's right to be concerned about Jackal. The man dotes on Allegra."

"Little girls have to grow up some time," I reminded them. "Besides, would he rather she fall for a boy she's known her entire life, one he knows will treat her right, or some unknown who could end up being an asshole?"

"Maybe I should let *you* tell Jackal about the kiss," Josie said. "You seem to have all the right answers."

I definitely did *not* have all the right answers. Writing happy endings made me feel a bit sappy when it came to relationships. Ones that weren't my own at any rate. The two young teens were sweet together. If Caleb already watched over Allegra, protected her, then it seemed to me he would be an amazing boyfriend for her. It's not like Jackal wouldn't know where to find him if the kid screwed up.

I pressed a hand to my stomach, wondering if Rooster and I would have a daughter or a son. They hadn't done an ultrasound yet. We hadn't even heard the heartbeat because an emergency had come up. At least the pregnancy had been confirmed, I'd been given a list of things I shouldn't eat or drink, and I was now on prenatal vitamins. Since I'd always been healthy, I was just using the over-the-counter ones.

"Aww. That's so cute," I said, pointing at Jordan and her three kids as they headed our way. Taggart had Salem up on his shoulders and Lanie had tucked her fingers into his belt.

"Don't let Lanie fool you. That girl is hell on wheels." Josie showed off a huge bruise on her calf. "She tackled me the other day, after hiding in the damn bushes."

Note to self, be on guard around Lanie. She looked so angelic right now. It was hard to believe she had horns hiding under her hair. I'd thought maybe she was misunderstood, but the bruise on Josie's leg was nearly black. If that girl came after me like that, I'd spank her ass whether her parents liked it or not. Someone needed to teach her manners.

"You ever want to see Cinder run, tell him Lanie is looking for him." Clarity smirked. "The tough old goat will take off so fast you'll only see a cloud of dust."

"I think I'd almost pay to see that," I said.

My phone chimed and I saw it was a text from Rooster. He knew I was hanging with the other old ladies today. I couldn't imagine what he'd want or need right now. I unlocked the phone to check the message.

Miss you.

Well, damn. Why did he have to be so sweet?

Miss you too. Be home in a bit.

Janessa groaned and put her hand over her mouth. She cast a frantic look around the area before bolting to some bushes. I winced at the sound of her puking. I seriously hoped she wasn't sick. The last thing I needed was picking up a bug. Even if I wasn't pressed to finish another book right now, I didn't want any setbacks. I already expected delays as my pregnancy advanced.

"Shit," Janessa said, retaking her seat. "Guess I can't keep it secret anymore."

Josie slid closer to me. "If you're contagious, get the hell away from me."

Janessa huffed at her. "I'm not sick, and thanks for the support, heifer."

Josie gaped but didn't respond.

"I'm pregnant." Janessa shot a glare my way. "I blame you! I thought I was done having kids, but no. You show up, knocked up by Rooster, and suddenly I'm having another baby."

Clarity's brow furrowed. "Didn't the doctor say you couldn't have more kids?"

"More like I *shouldn't* have more kids. I nearly bled out when I had Fiona. Which means they'll probably want to do a C-section with this baby. This is my last hurrah. My doctor said he wants me to take it easy. I really don't want to end up on bed rest, so Irish has threatened to lock me in a closet if I don't keep my ass home." Janessa looked a little green and ran for the bushes again.

"You aren't having morning sickness?" Josie asked.

I shook my head. So far, other than a missed period, I couldn't even tell I was pregnant. The tests I'd taken at home, and the one the doctor did at his office, all said there was a life growing inside me. If it weren't for that, I'd have thought I just skipped a month from all the stress I'd been under.

"Lucky bitch," Josie muttered. "I thought I was going to die with both pregnancies. Puking non-stop. It was awful."

Clarity looked at her kids. "I don't know. I think it's all worth it. Those babies are the most precious things in the world to me, except for their dad."

"Why didn't Meg come?" I asked. "Or Darby?"

"Darby is watching her kids and Meg's son. She wasn't sure she could contain them all at the playground, so she opted to stay home with them. As for Meg, she woke up with a sore throat and headache. She didn't want to chance getting anyone sick." Jordan shrugged. "I'd have brought them, but she said maybe next time."

"She's probably cuddled up next to Cinder binge watching TV," Josie said. "Since he stepped down as President, they've spent a lot of time together. I even saw him digging up the garden the other day and Meg was following along behind, prepping the soil. Next day, he helped her plant new flowers."

Jordan shook her head. "Man, never thought I'd see the day Cinder became so whipped. He was such a hard ass. Damn near missed out on having Meg in his life."

"I sense a story," I said.

"Oh, yeah. A good one," Janessa said as she rejoined us. "They almost died. It took someone literally putting a gun to his head for him to realize he was being a dumbass."

"Someone needs to tell me that one. I'd say we go out for drinks one night so you could spill all the club gossip, but sadly, I won't be drinking for a while. I miss wine. Like *really* miss it." I rubbed my stomach. "Rooster said he sees so much as one wine bottle in the house, he's going to shackle me to the bed until the baby is born."

Jordan wagged her eyebrows at me. "Tell him there are better uses for shackles than keeping you away from wine."

"I know, right?" I laughed. "So, is it just me, or does pregnancy make you want sex all the damn time? I found Rooster hiding in the pantry the other day. He'd heard me calling for him and panicked. When I yanked open the door, he grabbed the first thing he saw and crammed it in his mouth, pretending to have been searching for a snack."

"Seems reasonable enough," Josie said.

"He grabbed a garlic bulb." The girls burst out laughing. "On the plus side, if we have a sudden vampire invasion, they'll skip our house. I think that smell is still oozing from his pores."

"Okay, if no one else is going to bring it up, I will." Josie smacked her hand on the table. "When were you going to tell us the series was ending? What the hell, Alora?"

I shrugged. "They can't go on forever, you know. The Blogging Seductress series has apparently worn out its welcome with my publisher. Something about sales tapering off. They think readers have lost interest, so I have to pitch a new series. The next book I turn in will be the final in that series."

"Any ideas?" Clarity asked.

"I've always been known for writing Rom Coms, but I think I'd like to try something else. I'm just not sure my publisher will take something different. For me, writing is more of a cathartic process, a way to keep myself sane. For them, it's a numbers game. They invest money in my work and expect a return and then some. Can't say I blame them. If they threw money at stuff that bombed, they'd be out of business."

"Different how?" Jordan asked.

"After my experience with Officer Murray, I think I'd like to take on something more serious. Either a romantic suspense, or even a dark romance. I want to show the ugliness in the world, but still give the book a happy ending. A way to prove there's hope even in the darkest of times."

"Wow." Clarity smiled. "That's really awesome. I think if you pitched it to them just like that, you may be surprised by their answer. Doesn't hurt to try right? Maybe write up something for what you'd like to write and have a backup in case they reject the idea outright."

"I think I will." It was nice to have friends. These women might not be writers, but they still understood to some extent what I was going through. I'd explained how the publishing thing worked, how little say I had in certain aspects like price, covers, and to some degree even the content of my books. I had their support, and when I needed it most, they gave me an outlet for my frustration.

"I know the deadlines make you want to tear out your hair, and you said you tend to freak out over new releases, worried they'll tank. But anyone who talks to you about your books can tell you really love what you do," Clarity said.

"I do." My job was… everything. For me, it

wasn't a job so much as a calling. Even if I didn't have a publishing contract, or fans who adored my books, I'd still write. Deep down, I *had* to write. Stories came to me all the time. In addition to the notebook full of ideas, I also had another twenty partially written books in various genres. I didn't think I quite had what it took to write a mystery or horror novel, but it wouldn't stop me from trying. Didn't matter if it was never read by anyone other than me. At least I'd know I attempted it.

My phone chimed again.

You sure you're okay? Think it's almost half a day since you last begged for my cock.

I rolled my lips into my mouth to keep from laughing. Rooster wasn't wrong. By now, I'd have begged him to make me come a few times. Even though I felt the ache, the burning need, I was trying to be better about not unzipping his pants every other hour. Besides, I had a feeling he was getting a bit chafed. I'd noticed him wince when he walked to the bedroom last night.

"Let me guess. Rooster?" Jordan asked, nodding to my phone.

"Yep. He was amazed I've gone this long without sex."

Janessa snickered. "Maybe you should go home and take care of that. Poor guy. His dick might shrivel up and fall off. You could always offer to give it a kiss to make it all better."

I cracked up and wiped the tears from my eyes. "Oh, my God. I need to use that in the next book."

"Only if she's reviewing a pussy pocket in the shape of lips for her blog," Jordan said.

I laughed so hard my sides hurt. "Stop! I can't breathe!"

"Aww. Have you been giving Rooster a *hard* time?" Josie asked.

By the time we stopped giggling, I decided to call it a day and head home. It was bad enough I thought about sex all the damn time now. Thanks to these ladies, I now wanted to go home and ask Rooster if his dick needed a kiss. With some tongue.

Chapter Twelve
"Any marriage is hard work. But what I always say is, 'Keep the fights clean and the sex dirty.'"
-- Kevin Bacon

Rooster

The fact my woman got along with the other old ladies was great. Perfect. Even if it did mean she was hanging out with them right now instead of being here with me. I'd already flipped through the stations on TV. I'd even taken the dog out and tossed the ball for her. Charming didn't have any jobs for me to handle and had given me the day off. I'd imagined it having more sex and less "me" time.

The door opened and Alora hurried inside. She dropped her stuff in the entry and nearly ran to me. Before I could ask if she'd enjoyed herself, she'd pushed my knees apart and dropped down between them.

"Um, not that I'm complaining, but what you are..." She yanked my sweats down and nearly swallowed my cock. "Holy fuck!"

I fisted her hair, my heart trying to break its way out of my chest, as she sucked me so damn hard my eyes nearly rolled back in my head. Her nails bit into my thighs as she bobbed her head. Every time her lips touched the base of my cock, she swallowed. It felt like she was sucking my soul out of my body.

Her cheeks hollowed and she moaned as she worked me. A tingle started in my spine and my balls drew up. It only took one flick of her tongue and I was coming. I gripped her hair tighter, holding her still as I pumped into her mouth.

"Jesus, Alora!" I dragged her off me and she

licked her lips, looking pleased with herself. She had good reason. "What brought that on?"

"Well, one of the girls asked if I was giving you a hard time, and it made me think if you were hard and hurting, it was only fair that I ask if you wanted me to kiss it better, except I wanted to lick you too." She took a breath. "So when I got home, I was all worked up and needed your cock in my mouth."

"I fucking love you," I said, smiling at her.

"Yeah, yeah." She waved a hand. "You're only saying that because I just sucked you off."

I yanked her closer and kissed her hard. "No, I'm *especially* saying that because you ran in here like your ass was on fire, eager to suck my dick. But I'd love you even if you never sucked me off again."

She pressed her lips to mine then gave me a little nip. "No worries there. I love the way you taste. I'm addicted to the feel of you on my tongue. Just wish I could have your cock in my mouth and my pussy at the same time."

"Not unless you're a weird species of alien." I gave her a stern look. "And no, I'm not letting any other man put his dick in you. No matter how much you might get off on a threesome."

She winced. "After The Black Rose incident with Officer Murray, I think I prefer it just being the two of us. I don't want any creepy ass stalkers or rapists."

I ran my fingers along her jaw. "The club would never hurt you, but I don't like the idea of my brothers seeing you naked."

"One of them already did," she reminded me.

I nodded. "Yeah. Samurai did. So if you feel the need to have an audience again, I'll ask if he wants to come watch."

She fidgeted and I wondered what she was

thinking. I'd learned if I waited long enough, she'd tell me. I put my cock away and tugged her down onto my lap.

"When I first wanted to write my book series, I had a few ideas I played around with before settling on one." She took my hand and laced our fingers together. "Don't freak out, but… I tried a lot of the things in person to see if I was passionate enough about it to write a book based on whatever it was. One of the things on my list was being on a webcam show. The, um, erotic kind."

It really didn't surprise me to hear she'd tried something like that. What she'd done before we met wasn't anything I could hold against her. Hell, even if she'd done it after we'd met, I wouldn't have said shit.

"I wore a half-mask," she said. "In case I landed a publishing deal, I didn't want to ruin my chances by having a pornographic video of me floating around in cyberspace. And I used a stage name."

"Did you get off on it? Knowing a bunch of strangers were watching you?" I asked.

"Yeah. It's when I discovered I liked having people watch me get fucked. I never had anyone on the show with me. Just used toys on myself."

"You still have access to all that stuff? The webcam, the site you used…"

She nodded. "I haven't used it in years though. I'd just turned eighteen when I decided to try it. I'd have done it sooner, but they wouldn't let me."

Thank fuck for small favors. If there was kiddie porn out there featuring my woman, I'd have had to murder anyone who watched it.

"I have an idea." One I hoped didn't blow up in my fucking face, but I wanted my girl to have what she needed. Even if that meant other men watched her get off. "We'll set up a room upstairs with your webcam stuff, get whatever furniture and toys you need, and we'll both get disguises."

"Both?" she asked.

"Yep. If you're going to do this, I'm doing it with you. I just need to make sure all my ink is covered. You can wear a wig and a half-mask. I'll get a black domino or something to hide enough of my face I won't be easily recognized. Then you can get your webcam show set up again. Except this time, I'll be the one getting you off."

"But what about…" She placed a hand over her belly.

"You have a little time before you start to show. Once you get a baby bump, we'll shut it down. Or maybe I'll just record us for our personal collection instead. Might be fun."

She shifted until she straddled me. "You'd really do all that for me? I know how you feel about sharing me."

"Not really sharing, baby girl. You're still mine and only mine. Letting someone else watch isn't the same as them touching you. Way I see it, marriage is about compromise. I saw the way you reacted when Samurai joined us, and again at The Black Rose. I'm not going to take that away from you because I'm a possessive asshole."

"I feel like I'm the only one getting something from this."

I hugged her tighter. "I already have what I wanted most. You. I didn't have to chase you near as much I'd thought I would. You're the greatest gift I could ever receive, Alora. You and our kid. Long as I have the two of you, nothing else matters."

She squirmed on my lap. "Think you're ready for

round two yet?"

"Only if I get to make you come multiple times first."

"I'd have to be stupid to say no to that," she said. "Multiple O's? Sign me up!"

She hopped off my lap and took off upstairs. I followed, taking a moment to make sure the dog was still in the yard. My brothers had helped put up a six-foot fence to keep Gypsy in, except she'd escaped twice. The dog was sprawled in the grass, sunning herself like a damn cat. Her water dish still looked half-full, so I decided to leave her be.

By the time I got upstairs, Alora had stripped out of her clothes and lay spread-eagle on the bed. She'd even pulled out a handful of toys and had them lined up down the edge of the mattress, and the bottle of lube on the nightstand. She didn't know I'd bought a few things to supplement the large collection we already had. As much as I wanted to try them all, I didn't want to use everything today. I ducked into one of the empty rooms and grabbed the foam wedge I'd had delivered this morning.

"On your knees, middle of the bed, and face the headboard," I said.

She complied immediately, her eyes lighting up when she saw what I had in my hands. I put the wedge on the bed and positioned her over it, just the way I wanted her. I used the Velcro restraints on the headboard, making sure they were snug enough she couldn't escape.

I took the silk blindfold out of the bedside table drawer and covered her eyes. I wanted her to use her other senses. It always heightened her pleasure. I trailed my fingers down her spine to her ass and gave it a smack, leaving a pink mark on her pale skin.

Quiet as I could, I got my camera from my dresser drawer and took a few pictures of her. I nudged her thighs apart, spreading her pussy open, and snapped two more. Then I placed it across the room and set it to video. It wasn't something I'd ever share with anyone, or let her post online, but I thought she might like watching it with me later.

"Ready, baby girl?"

"For you? Always."

I smiled and picked up the large vibrating plug, surprised she'd chosen that one. She usually preferred one a bit smaller. I lubed the toy, then dripped some down the crack of her ass and started working my finger into her tight hole.

"Feel good?" I asked.

"You're teasing me!" She wiggled her ass. "You know I can handle more than that."

"Really? You sure? Don't want more prep?"

She hesitated. "I don't know. Are you putting your cock in there?"

"No. At least, not right now."

"Then no, I don't need more prep. Show me what you've got!"

I eased the plug into her ass and turned it on, setting the vibration to a medium speed. She squealed at first, but it quickly turned to a soft moan. Yeah, my girl liked having her ass played with. I knew she liked her spankings too. I'd get to that in a minute.

"Did you know your special egg does something rather fun?" I asked.

"Like make me come a lot?"

I smacked her ass. Hard. "No. I can set it to vibrate in time with music."

I inserted the egg and synced to the app on my phone. After finding a song with a lot of bass, I let the toys do their job while I had fun playing with my woman. She squirmed and begged, pleaded with me to let her come. I knew she'd ride the edge until I touched her clit.

I got onto the bed behind her, arching my body over hers. My cock slid along her wet slit and I rocked against her a few times. Her breath caught and I knew she was waiting, hoping I'd let her come.

I worked my hand between her torso and the wedge, giving her nipple a sharp pinch. Alora yelped and jolted under me.

"Too much?" I asked.

"Not enough. More! Do it again."

I gave the distended tip a tug before twisting and pinching it some more. I slid my hand to her other breast and worked that side, making her a hot, needy mess. I rocked against her again, the head of my cock bumping her clit with every stroke.

"Oh, God! Killian! I'm so close."

"I know, baby girl. I know." I tugged on her nipple again. "Come for me. Show me how much you want my dick."

She pressed back against me as I continued toying with her. She yanked at the restraints, a sob catching in her throat. Sweat slicked her body and I knew she wouldn't last much longer. I leaned over her more, putting my lips by her ear, my chest to her back, and pressing tighter against the plug in her ass. She cried out and tensed.

"That's it. Get my cock wet, dirty girl. Come all over me."

A loud keening sound escaped her as she thrust back against me. I pulled my hips far enough away to remove the egg from her pussy before driving into her balls deep. She screamed as her pussy clenched down on my dick, her orgasm rolling into another one. I rode her hard, my hips slapping against her. The wedge braced her enough I could give her a good, hard fucking and it would keep her pinned in place beneath me. Knowing she couldn't move, that she was at my mercy, heightened the pleasure. Even better was the knowledge she fucking loved it.

I bellowed as I came, thrusting into her harder. I didn't stop until every drop had been wrung from me, her pussy full of my cum. My chest heaved as I tried to catch my breath. My cock twitched and fuck me if it wasn't still hard. I leaned back and removed the plug from her ass and reached for the large dildo she'd set out. I should have been jealous of the monster sized dick, especially since it had been created from the mold of an actual porn star's junk.

I worked it into her ass before I started fucking her again. I didn't think I could come a second time, not this fast, but she felt so damn good.

"Want me to fuck your ass?" I asked.

"Fuck me hard, Killian. Treat me like your dirty little whore."

And now my dick was even harder. I loved when she talked like that. I used the dildo to fuck her ass. Long, deep strokes that had her pleading for more. I didn't hold out long before I started thrusting into her pussy. When she came, she managed to pull another orgasm from me. A small one. I wasn't sure I'd have anything left to give her, at least not for the rest of the day.

I pulled the dildo from her ass and slipped free of her body. I kissed my way down her spine before giving her hip a bite. Leaning back, I spread her open and watched my cum slip out of her.

"Beautiful," I murmured.

"You say that every time."

"And I mean it. My cum smeared across your pussy and coating your thighs isn't something I'll ever tire of seeing."

"Killian?"

"What, baby girl?"

"If you aren't going to give me more orgasms, we should probably clean up."

"Christ, woman! Aren't you exhausted?"

She shook her head. "No. Still really horny."

I looked through the toys she'd pulled out and spotted the one I knew she needed right now. It was U-shaped and the thick part went in her pussy while the smaller bulbous end fit over her clit. I slid it into place and turned it on, setting it as high as it would go. I curled my body over hers, nibbling on her shoulders and neck.

I lost track of how many more times she came, but when I heard a soft snore from her, I shut off the toy and set everything in the bathroom to be cleaned. I freed Alora from the blindfold and restraints, eased her off the wedge, and put it back in the spare room. Once everything had been put away, and the camera had been shut off, I crawled into bed next to her, holding her while she slept.

I'd never met a woman with as big a sexual appetite as my wife, and I knew I was a lucky bastard. It was like having my own personal porn star. I loved how adventurous she was, how open, and I definitely liked the way she sucked my cock. I couldn't imagine finding a woman more perfect for me.

"Love you," I whispered and kissed her forehead.

She murmured in her sleep and snuggled closer. I started to close my eyes and my phone rang. I grabbed it before the sound would wake her and answered.

"Rooster."

"No shit," Charming said. "Wanted to give you a heads up. The Demonic Reign chapter you buddied up to has been wiped out. There's rumblings there could be more of them further north in Nevada and Montana. I'm bringing our boys home, but the Savage Knights and Mayhem Riders said they'd take it from here. We're in the clear."

"Good. One less ax waiting to take off my head."

"Enjoy the rest of your day off."

Before I could say anything else, Charming had hung up. I placed the phone on the bedside table and cuddled my woman. It looked like I didn't have to worry about those men trying to track me down. Alora was safe, at least for now. I couldn't say whether or not other trouble would find us, but the Demonic Reign weren't an issue anymore, and neither was Officer Murray.

Life was pretty fucking sweet at the moment.

Epilogue
"A gentleman holds my hand. A man pulls my hair.
A soulmate will do both."
        -- Alessandra Torre

Alora

I stared at the screen of the ultrasound machine, knowing my eyes and ears must be playing tricks on me. "I'm sorry, could you repeat that. I thought you said it was quadruplets."

The technician grinned like she'd just told me I won the lottery, and not that my pussy would never be the same again. *Four* kids? They'd rip me open, and the doctor would never be able to stitch me up tight enough. Rooster would go to the club for pussy because his dick would fall out when he tried to put it in me.

I turned my gaze on my husband, who rocked back on his heels and looked a bit poleaxed. "This is *your* fucking fault! Quads don't run my family. Only twins."

"There's four," he muttered, looking a little green. "Four."

The technician nodded. "Yep. Hard to say for sure, but it looks like they might be girls. I stress the word *might*."

Why hadn't I been back to the doctor for my scheduled appointments? Oh,right. I'd decided fucking Rooster was a better idea and missed the last two. So here we were, six months into my pregnancy, and finding out we were having *four* babies. *Four. My. Life.*

"You're only getting anal after this," I said.

The technician choked and turned red before hurrying out of the room with a quick, "I'll give you two a moment."

"You like my dick in your ass," he said.

"Yeah, but you better not shove anything in my pussy that isn't plastic after these kids get here. I'm never doing this again. You hear me? *Never*."

"It did take two of us to knock you up. It's not like you were passed out and didn't have a say in the matter. You wanted me to fuck you."

I nodded. "I did. I still do. But only in my ass. Oh, and my mouth. I'll suck you off anytime you want. In fact, I'll do it right now."

He danced back out of reach. "We are *not* having sex in the middle of your ultrasound."

My hand trembled and tears welled in my eyes. I reached for him. "Killian, I'm scared."

He gripped my fingers and ran his other hand over my hair. "We've got this, Alora. So it's more than we'd bargained for. You know you're going to love these babies. You already do. And so do I. We have a big family to help us if we get overwhelmed. Just take a breath."

I nodded. "All right. I'm sorry I threatened you."

"I wouldn't exactly call it a threat that you offered to suck me off whenever I wanted and let me fuck your ass. I enjoy both those things."

Another horrifying thought occurred to me. "The webcam show. We can't do it when this is all over."

His brow furrowed. "Why not? I mean, it won't be easy having any alone time with four babies in the house, but we can find a way."

"They're going to wreck my pussy," I wailed and started bawling.

I had to give Rooster credit. He might have laughed silently, his chest vibrating under my cheek as he hugged me, but at least he didn't do it out loud. If he had, I may have been a widow. I was ninety-nine percent certain Scratch had meant it when he said he'd help me bury the body. We had the best friends ever.

"Love you, baby girl. You are the most amazing, beautiful woman I know. And now you're giving me not one but four kids. I'll be here by your side, every step of the way."

The technician came back in, looking like I may have scarred her for life. Clearly she needed a copy of one of my books. If me talking about anal had spooked her that much, she needed help. A sex-tervention. Wait. Was that a thing? If not, it should be.

"Rooster, would you get the book from the side of my bag?" I asked.

He pulled out the copy I carried around in case I found a new reader or a fan. I handed it to the tech, who stared at it like it might bite her.

"Let's start slow. This is a book. You turn the pages and read the little squiggles on them, called words. This one has lots of sexy stuff in it. You might learn something. Like how to not be a frigid bitch. Your boyfriend will thank me later."

The woman gaped at me, her face turning redder by the minute.

Rooster sighed and I knew he thought I'd gone too far, but really. The woman clearly needed help. It was my civic duty to make sure she learned about multiple orgasms, and the joy of blowjobs.

"On that note, my wife needs to shut up." I glared at him and stuck out my tongue. His eyes heated and he smirked. "You can use that later."

The tech squeaked and I just knew she'd run and hide the next time we had an appointment. Rooster couldn't very well scold me when he was just as bad.

"Can we tell what the babies are?" he asked.

"Human, I hope," I muttered.

He squeezed my hand to get me to be quiet.

The tech moved the wand around my belly. It took a bit of maneuvering, but she managed to tell the sex of two, but the other two weren't being cooperative.

"Well, I'd thought they were all girls, but it seems I was wrong. This bigger one is a boy. The smallest is a girl. We'll have to check next time for the other two. Congratulations!"

She printed off a few pictures for us to keep and cleaned the goop off my belly. It wasn't long before we'd set my next appointment and were back in the truck.

Four. Babies.

"You realize life as we know it just ended," I said. "Better sleep and fuck as much as we can now. Once these rug rats get here, we won't have a moment of peace until they move out. I'll get cobwebs down there. My clit will shrivel up and fall off."

Rooster snorted. "Baby girl, even if I have to fuck you in the shower, we aren't going eighteen years without sex. It's called multi-tasking."

"All right, but if you're going to fuck me while I'm washing dishes, you'd better invest in unbreakable plates. I won't be responsible for what happens otherwise."

"Taking you from behind in front of the sink?" He eyed me. "We can give it a try when we get home."

Rooster pulled over into the parking lot of my favorite restaurant and we went inside. Even though it didn't seem busy, no one stood at the hostess stand.

I laughed and shook my head. "That poor technician. I think we've scared her off. She'll see we're coming in and run away."

"Maybe she'll read your book."

"Yeah well, if it changes her life, she better at least name her dog after me. It's the least she can do. I mean, who wouldn't want to experience multiple orgasms?"

"I think you have sex on the brain too much."

I folded my arms. "Did you know the *Journal of Sex Research* determined men think about sex nineteen times a day? If you can think about it that much, then I can too."

"Fair enough. Just maybe not discuss it in public next time. You're going to give some sweet elderly lady a heart attack one of these days."

A throat cleared behind us. "Young man, just because women get old, doesn't mean we don't still like sex."

I turned to see a petite silver-haired lady behind me, and her husband. They stood with their arms linked, and a twinkle in their eyes. The smirk on her lips told me she'd been a troublemaker in her youth, and quite possibly still was.

The hostess returned and took us to a table. Rooster shivered as he slid into the booth.

"What?" I asked.

"I need brain bleach."

"For what?"

"The mental image of that woman having sex. Quick! Tell me something to take my mind off it."

"Four. Kids. Four screaming, snotty kids who will never let us sleep again."

His shoulders relaxed. "Thanks, that did the trick. Now I'm horrified for another reason."

"Could be worse," I said.

"How?"

"They could all be like Lanie."

Rooster yelled out for our server. "I need a beer! No, bring two pitchers."

I snickered. My life hadn't turned out the way I'd planned, but then how did you *plan* for someone like Rooster? I adored him, and I couldn't wait to spend the rest of our lives together. He was perfect for me in every way. Except for the part where his swimmers put four babies in me at the same time.

But he'd been right. We'd figure it out. No matter how scary it was to think of fucking up the lives of four tiny humans, as long as Rooster was beside me, nothing else mattered. We could take on the world as long as we did it together.

Who'd have thought having an IRS auditor and cop show up at my house would end up being the best thing to happen to me? Not only had I won the battle over writing off the sex toys, but I'd found my other half, the man destined to be mine. I'd never complain about filing taxes ever again. Well, I wouldn't complain *too* much.

Cuffs & Kink (A Bad Boy Romance)
Harley Wylde

Ty: It was no secret I was a manwhore and enjoyed my fair share of women. More than one woman had tried to pin me down over the years, but no way was the noose of matrimony slipping around my neck. I was a fuck 'em and leave 'em kind of guy, and I liked my life just the way it was. Badge bunnies fell into my bed in droves, even the ones who liked to play innocent, but there was one type of woman I'd always avoided -- virgins. Which makes things a little awkward when hot little Josie Wright, the reverend's daughter, makes me harder than I've ever been before. Just one look at those slender legs and perky tits and all I can think about is being balls deep inside of her, but good girls like Josie don't hang out with bad boys like me.

Josie: I've always had the perfect life -- loving parents and a stable home life. Until now. When my father told me I was to marry Reverend Falks, a man thirty years my senior, in exchange for our church getting a new roof, I was sure he had to be kidding, but the good reverend has told me in no uncertain terms that he plans to keep me barefoot and pregnant, along with some other details that make my stomach queasy. I'll do anything to avoid my fate, even if it means falling into Officer Ty Daniels' bed. Except once I'm there, I don't want to leave. He makes me feel things I've never experienced before, and for the first time in my life I'm realizing that maybe it's good to be a little bad.

Chapter One

Ty

Holy fuck! It had obviously been too long since I'd gotten laid if little Josie Wright had my dick standing at attention. She couldn't be more than twenty, and her prim and proper attire always made her look even younger. At least, that was normally the case, but it seemed the reverend's daughter was taking a walk on the wild side in her short shorts and barely-there halter top. How the hell had she escaped her parents' house looking like that?

She normally looked more like a boy than a woman, but fuck if those shorts didn't hug slender curves. The shirt was molded to her, showing off breasts that looked perky even if they were on the small side. I'd always been into stacked women, but for some reason those understated curves of hers were making me harder than hell.

I needed to avert my eyes and get my monster cock under control. Walking around town with my dick tenting my uniform trousers was probably not a good idea. I was pretty sure if anyone knew it was Josie who'd given me wood, I'd be run out of town by the end of the day. Hell, I had to be a dozen years her senior, but fuck if my dick cared right now. Had she really been hiding that body all this time? I glanced her way again and saw her talking to some of the boys from the local college. She was better off with someone closer to her age, even if I did want to bend her over the hood of that little VW Beetle she tooled around in every day. That ivory skin of hers would look hot against the cherry red paint.

She laughed at something they said and the sound carried on the breeze. It reminded me of damn fairies, it was so light. My cock jerked against my zipper, and I discreetly adjusted myself. If I didn't get the hell back into my cruiser and away from Josie, I was going to end up embarrassing myself. Hell, I was already embarrassed that a slip of a woman had me harder than I'd ever been before. And knowing that prim and proper Josie was more than likely a virgin just made matters worse. I'd always steered clear of innocent women, but I would have loved to corrupt her. An image of her bound to my bed flashed in my mind, and I groaned as I reached for my cock again.

I was just about to slide into my vehicle when the tone of her voice changed. Her harsh, urgent tones had me turning her way again. One of the guys had her hands shackled behind her in his massive grip while the other leaned into her space. When I saw him fondle her breasts and her struggle to break free, I found myself slamming the car door and charging down the street. His lips were on her neck as his hands pawed at her, and without thought I reached out and grabbed him by the back of his neck, slamming him facedown onto the back of her Beetle.

"I believe Miss Wright said no."

"What the fuck, man?" the dickhead whined. "We were just having some fun."

"I suggest you have fun somewhere else, because if I catch you having that kind of fun in my town again I'm hauling your asses to jail for attempted rape. I have no doubt that's where you intended to take things. Maybe not here in the middle of the street, but once you'd managed to get her alone. Isn't that right?"

The second guy held his hands in the air and backed away. "It was just a bit of fun, officer. She's not worth the trouble."

The one in my grasp struggled to break free, but I

slammed him against the car again. His face was turning almost the same color as her paint job, and I smiled grimly. Josie looked at me with wide eyes as she massaged her wrists. I saw the angry red marks where they'd held her too tight, and it made me want to lash out at the asshole in my grip.

"What do you say, Miss Wright? Are you pressing charges? I doubt I could nail them for attempted rape, but definitely for assault."

She shook her head, and I noticed her eyes were shiny with unshed tears. Fuck me. My heart twisted in my chest at that innocent face looking so crushed. If she'd known what would happen, I'm betting she wouldn't have worn those clothes outside of her house today. Hell, I was the law and even I was hard as a fence post just looking at her. Men should be able to control themselves better, and most of us could. A woman had every right to wear whatever she wanted. But there was always a dickhead in the bunch. Or in this case, two.

"Looks like you're free to go, asshole, but steer clear of Josie. You hear me?"

I released him, and he took off down the street without even a backward glance. I wouldn't be surprised if he'd pissed himself at some point. Once I was certain he was gone and wouldn't cause more problems, I turned to face Josie. Before I could even open my mouth to ask if she was okay, she launched herself into my arms, plastering that sweet body against me. Yeah, if I'd been hard before, I was a fucking steel post now. There was no way she didn't feel the effects of her body against mine. Surely, even Josie Wright wasn't that innocent.

"Thank you, Officer Daniels. I thought they were harmless, but…"

My shirt felt suspiciously damp, and I looked down to see tears streaking her cheeks. My arms tightened around her as I did my best to comfort her, without copping a feel. I might be an ass, but I wasn't that much of an ass. Although, *her* ass... No, I wasn't going to think about her ass, even if it did look good enough to bite.

"Let's get you home," I said, setting her away from me -- or trying to. The damn woman was attached like a barnacle. Her arms tightened around my waist, and I expected her to wrap her legs around me too.

Mmmm. Oh yeah, arms around my neck, legs around my waist. Now that was an image I could jerk off to later. Sweet little Josie, open and willing and oh so wet. I'd bet she tasted divine and felt even better. Not that I would ever find out. Nope. I was going to put her in my car and take her home where her mama could take care of her.

Maybe I was a glutton for punishment. She did have her car with her. The smarter thing to do would have been following her home. Unfortunately, I wasn't thinking with the head on my shoulders, and the little head (although, to be honest, it really wasn't little -- just sayin') was all for spending more time with Josie. I tucked her into my cruiser before sliding behind the wheel. Her scent filled the small space, and I couldn't help but admire just how far those shorts rode up when she was sitting down. If they were any tinier, they'd have been panties. Was she wearing any panties?

I gave myself a mental slap and backed the car out of the space.

"I'll drop you by your parents' home, and you can arrange to get your car later."

"I don't want to go there."

I stopped at a four-way intersection and looked at her. "Then where do you want to go?"

"Can we just drive around for a bit?"

Holy hell. She was trying to kill me. Or get me fired, because I was pretty sure the police chief wouldn't be too pleased to find me balls deep inside Josie Wright on the side of the road, and if she stayed in this car much longer, that was what would happen.

"Josie, I don't think that's a good idea."

She blinked at me innocently before her gaze dropped to my lap, and my very hard cock. Her eyes dilated and her lips parted. The way she licked her lips was enough to make my dick jerk, and I knew I had to get her out of the car and away from me as fast as possible. Either that or I was going to be very, very bad.

"Josie." My tone came out strangled as she continued to stare.

Her cheeks flushed, and her eyes cut toward the window. I could tell she was intrigued, yet her innocence kept her from saying what was on her mind. And hell if that didn't just turn me on even more. I'd been with more women than I could count, but damn if she didn't make me harder than I'd ever been before. But Josie wasn't a "right now" kind of woman. She was the forever kind. I might have been thirty-two, but I wasn't ready for the picket fence, golden retriever in the yard, and two point five kids just yet. No, whoever plucked her cherry was going to be a lucky bastard, but I'd be willing to bet it would be her husband.

"Why don't you want to go home?" I asked. She'd always been around town with one of her parents, seldom on her own, so something had to be going on. It wasn't like Josie to dress like this or refuse to go home.

She stared at the window and didn't say a word.

"Josie, if you don't give me a good reason, I'm going to take you home right now. You were attacked, and you should talk to someone, preferably your mother."

She snorted.

"Talk to me."

She turned those wide blue eyes my way and looked completely lost and betrayed. Hurting Josie was akin to kicking a puppy. Whatever put that look in her eyes, or *whoever*, I felt the need to lash out at them and beat them bloody. She should be cherished and treated like a princess. Whatever had happened, that one look told me she'd been cut deep.

"They're selling me."

Well, I hadn't expected that.

"I think you need to clarify that statement. What do you mean they're selling you? Last time I checked, slavery was illegal."

She sighed. "My father has a friend, a minister in another town, who wants a young, pure wife. Someone to give him a dozen kids and teach Sunday school every weekend. A woman who won't talk back or ever voice her own opinion. And he's old! Like at least fifty."

I stifled my smile at that. Fifty was hardly old, but to someone her age it probably seemed ancient.

"And your father is urging you to marry this man?" I asked.

"It's worse. My father has promised him that he can have me. In exchange, our church is getting a new roof. Reverend Falks has a large congregation, one of those super churches that brings in millions. The man lives in a castle, for cripes sake!"

"And all that luxury doesn't appeal to you?"

Her lips twisted. "Would you want to sleep with a man thirty years older than you for the express purpose of being a brood mare? Reverend Falks doesn't believe in birth control and he already informed me that he plans for me to stay barefoot and pregnant. He's told me what he intends to do to me, and it makes my skin crawl. He's cruel, but the world only sees a kind man who lost his first wife too young. What they don't know is that he probably killed her."

Those were strong allegations, and I wondered how much was spoken in fear and how much was truth. I wasn't overly familiar with Falks. I never watched his sermons on Sunday morning, but I knew he was a big shot around these parts. And if he had decided he wanted Josie, there probably wasn't much she could do about it. She was dependent on her family with no way of supporting herself. And in a town this small, the law wasn't always on her side.

Luckily for her, I was.

My uncle was the local judge, and my cousins all worked for the department like me. I wasn't sure there was anything we could do to protect Josie, but I'd be damned if I wouldn't at least try. I flipped a U-turn and headed for the courthouse. If anyone could figure out this mess, it was Judge Turner.

"Where are we going?" she asked.

"We're going to pay a visit to my uncle and see if he has an idea of how to get you out of this mess. They aren't technically doing anything illegal -- yet -- but they can't force you to marry someone you don't want. The marriage isn't legal unless you both say 'I do' and I guess you don't intend to do that."

"If I refuse, I'll be thrown out of the house. I've never attended college and don't have a job. How would I pay for a place to live?"

"One thing at a time, Josie."

She sighed and settled back against the seat. When we reached the courthouse, she reached out and gripped my hand tight. The jolt I felt was enough to momentarily stun me, but I snapped out of it and ushered her through the building and to the judge's chambers. He had an open door policy for family, and I hoped like hell he wasn't hearing any court cases. The sooner I helped Josie figure out her problem, the sooner I could put some distance between us. Before I did something embarrassing.

As it happened, Judge Turner was in, and he seemed to be in a good mood.

"Well, if it isn't my favorite nephew!" He pounded me on the back.

"I'm your only nephew," I said wryly.

"Semantics. Now, why have you brought pretty Josie Wright with you? Don't tell me you're finally settling down."

My eyes widened, but my mouth refused to work.

"Officer Daniels thinks you might be able to help me, Your Honor."

"I'm off duty. Call me Mr. Turner." My uncle smiled fondly at her. "Now, what seems to be the trouble, Josie?"

She told him the same story she'd shared with me, and when she was finished, my uncle was frowning. He paced the length of his office before stopping in front of us, hands on hips. His lips were pursed, and I could tell he was measuring his words before he said anything. He was always the type to think before he spoke, even when answering a curious eight-year old's questions.

"Well, Ty could run you over to the women's shelter, if they've got room, but that's just a temporary solution. I'm guessing you'd have a hard time finding a job and a place to live around here once Reverend Falks puts the word out he's looking for you. You could leave town, but I'm thinking you don't have family anywhere else who'd take you in, and eventually Falks would catch up with you." Josie didn't say anything, but we both knew my uncle was right. There was the law, then there was the reality of a small southern town. "I think it's obvious what needs to happen."

"And that is?" I asked.

"Josie needs to lose her virginity."

I stared at him, fairly certain I'd misheard. There was no way that was his only thought on the matter, which meant he was up to something. "You think losing her virginity will make a difference?"

He shrugged. "Reverend Falks wants a pure wife, so if she loses her virginity she won't be pure anymore. He should lose interest and move on to someone else."

Josie frowned. "I haven't heard of any male prostitutes in town, so just how am I supposed to lose my virginity before I go home today?"

I coughed and sputtered. "Pardon? Did you just say you were going to use a male prostitute?"

"Well, what else am I supposed to do? I'm too young to hit the local bars, and even if I did, I can't very well take someone home with me. And who in this town is going to deflower the reverend's daughter? Aside from those jerks earlier, I'm pretty untouchable in most peoples' eyes."

"Trust me, plenty of men around here want to touch you," I muttered.

My uncle laughed because the state of my arousal wasn't easily hidden. Despite the fury I'd felt when she'd told me her parents were trading her for a roof for their church, I'd remained pretty damn hard. It was difficult to get myself under control with her so near, especially when she smelled incredible.

"Why don't I give a call to the police chief and tell him you're taking the rest of the day off?" my uncle suggested. "You can take Josie to your place and discuss her issue further."

The knowing look in his eyes had heat creeping up my neck and settling in my cheeks. I was a grown ass man, but talking about sex with my uncle could still reduce me to a hormonal twelve-year-old boy who'd asked him about the birds and the bees. And fuck me if he hadn't just put Josie right where I'd wanted her -- in my bed.

If she understood what was going on, she didn't let on. Those innocent eyes studied me as if she were waiting for me to make a decision. Virgin or not, she knew I wanted her, and my uncle was throwing her into my arms. If she had a problem with that, she kept quiet.

I sighed and tipped my head toward the door. "Come on. I'll take you to my place and we can figure this out."

She gave me a slight smile, but her eyes warmed and her cheeks flushed. My chest ached with how beautiful she was, and it seemed that at least for the next few hours, she was mine. Fuck me if that didn't please me more than it should. Something told me this would come back to bite me in the ass, but until then, I was going to have one very happy dick.

Chapter Two

Josie

I'd be lying if I said I wasn't nervous, extremely nervous, but then handsome men always did that to me. Officer Ty Daniels definitely was a handsome man. It hadn't escaped my attention just how well he filled out that uniform, with his biceps bulging against the sleeves of his shirt. I felt tingles in places that had long lain dormant, and despite my nerves, I felt a bit of excitement over being alone with him.

"Officer Daniels…"

"Call me Ty."

Ty. It suited him. "Ty, are you going to lose your job for helping me?"

"Doubt it. If my chief knew what your parents were up to, he'd be the first one to step in. I should warn you, my place is a bit of a mess right now. I've been pulling extra shifts, so I haven't had much time for housekeeping."

"I'm sure your place is fine."

How messy could it possibly be? I'd heard bachelor pads could be horrendous, but I'd never actually seen one. My parents' home was always pristine. My father wouldn't have it any other way, and if my mother didn't keep a tidy home, then she paid the price. Not that anyone would ever believe that Reverend Wright would dare beat his family. If only people knew the truth. I'd wanted to escape for a while, but until I found a job it wouldn't be possible. And if my father put the word out that he didn't want me working, then no one would hire me.

Ty pulled into the driveway of a small brick home with blue shutters and a maple door. I hadn't known what to expect of Ty's home, but it looked quainter than I'd thought it would. I'd honestly thought maybe he lived in one of the two apartment complexes in town. A home made him seem more settled, though I had a feeling that wasn't a word he would use to describe himself.

I followed him up to the front door and slipped inside behind him. He shut off the alarm and motioned for me to have a seat. His furniture was chocolate leather and a large TV dominated one wall. It had to be at least sixty inches or more. My father didn't really believe in the evils of TV, unless it was a religious program, so we had one small set in our living room and he ruled the remote with an iron fist.

The leather of the sofa creaked as I sank onto a cushion.

"Do you want anything to drink? I think I have some soda and some bottled water, or I could make a pot of coffee."

Ty looked nervous, and I wondered if this was just as awkward for him as it was for me. I knew Ty's uncle hoped his nephew would rid me of my virginity, and I wouldn't mind Ty being the one to take it. Honestly, he was hotter than any of the guys I'd seen around town, but I'd always thought he saw me as a little girl since he was older than me. I wasn't sure how much older, but I knew he'd dated women in their thirties. I'd seen him here and there with one beauty after another hanging on his arm. Not that I'd been stalking him, but he was hard not to notice.

"Ty, you don't have to do this. I know your uncle thinks it's best if I lose my virginity, but I don't want you to feel like you have to help me. He wasn't very subtle when he suggested I come home with you."

He smirked. "Honey, getting it up isn't going to be a problem, but I've never been with a virgin before and I'm not sure I have enough finesse for something like that."

I rubbed my hands against my thighs and stood up. "I never said I wanted finesse."

"And what is it you want?"

I moved a little closer to him, the heat of his body pressing against me. "You could start by kissing me."

His gaze skated down my body. "And if I don't want to stop at just a kiss?"

"Isn't that why I'm here?"

Ty reached out and wove his fingers through my hair, tilting my head back as he urged my body closer. My breasts pressed against his chest, the cool metal of his badge making my nipples harden. My lips parted as I waited for him to make his move. I'd never told anyone before, but I'd never been kissed. Being held against him was the closest I'd ever come to being kissed, to being embraced by someone other than family, and a thrill ran through me.

His head lowered and his mouth brushed against mine, leaving my lips tingling from the contact. I felt his tongue swipe against my lower lip and I let him in, reveling in the taste and feel of him. Our tongues tangled and I molded my body to his, his cock digging into my belly. I'd never seen a naked man before, and until this moment I'd never much cared one way or another about it. But suddenly, I wanted to see Ty in all his naked glory, and I knew without a doubt that it would be spectacular. The muscles in his body were hard and unyielding against my softer curves. My panties grew damp as he ravaged my mouth, his lips and tongue taking pleasure as well as giving it.

I shifted my hands up over his chest and reached for the buttons on his uniform. I popped them free, one at a time, and felt frustrated when I realized there was another shirt underneath. I had no idea how to unclip the belt that held his gun and other things like handcuffs. A shiver raked my spine as I wondered if he'd use the cuffs on me. I might be a virgin, but I'd read enough romance novels to have a few ideas about what I'd like to experience.

Ty broke away, his breathing heavy and his gaze hungry.

"This is your last chance to change your mind, Josie. I don't think I'll be able to stop if this goes any further. I may be strong, but I'm not that damn strong."

I smiled a little, feeling a thrill of power that he wanted me that much. It made me wonder if a powerful man like Ty would fall to his knees with the right touch, the right kiss, the right words. I had none of those right now, but I would learn.

"I want this, Ty. I want you," I told him, and I meant every word. I'd never been tempted before now, but standing here in his house with him so near, I knew without a doubt that I wanted him to be the one to claim my virginity.

Ty swung me into his arms and carried me down the hall to the bedroom. He kicked open the door and set me on the edge of the bed as he made quick work of shedding his uniform. I watched, hungry and yearning for things I'd only ever read about, as each item of clothing hit the floor. My mouth ran dry at the sight of his impressive cock, hard and ready. I had nothing to compare him to, but he seemed rather large, and I wondered if he was going to fit. Compared to his height of six foot three, I was rather small at barely five feet tall. Our size difference hadn't mattered to me, but the monster that seemed eager to get inside of me did worry me a bit.

"I won't lie," Ty said. "I've heard it hurts the first time, and I'm not exactly small. Not as huge as some, but I have a good eight inches here that I'm hoping will make you scream in pleasure."

"Just... go slow."

He nodded.

I stood and awkwardly stripped out of my clothes, my cheeks burning. No one had ever seen me naked before except my mother and my doctor. I wasn't exactly blessed when it came to boobs, but I hoped what I had was adequate. As hard as he was, he didn't seem to mind my smaller curves. I'd seen the women he usually dated -- not that this was a date -- and they looked like goddesses with curves that Aphrodite would envy.

"Have you ever touched yourself?" he asked.

My cheeks flamed hotter, and I shook my head. I'd thought about it, plenty of times, but our walls at home were thin and I'd worried about making any noises my parents might hear.

"I'm going to touch you, Josie, and I want you to tell me if you don't like something. Okay? I want you to enjoy this as much as you can. If something doesn't feel right or hurts, you speak up."

"O-okay."

Ty came closer, his hands cupping my shoulders and sliding down my arms. Goosebumps rose along my skin from his touch. He knelt in front of me, putting him at eye level with me. His hands came up my sides, skimming over my ribs, to cup my breasts. They were barely a handful, but the look in his eyes said he didn't mind. If anything he seemed to like exploring my body, and I couldn't wait for him to do more.

His lips closed over the tip of one breast. Sparks

of pleasure shot from my nipple to my core, and I couldn't stifle the gasp that rose to my lips. Ty moved to the other side as his hands slid down to cup my hips. His mouth burned against my skin as he kissed his way down the valley of my breasts and across my stomach. His palms cupped my ass and lifted me, placing me on the edge of the bed. My thighs parted, giving him room to move between them.

Ty shifted, focusing on my legs. He kissed and nipped up my thighs until he'd made his way to my pussy. Even though I'd never been intimate with someone before, I'd shaved since I'd turned sixteen and read my first romance novel. Shaving had seemed sexy, and I'd wanted desperately to be sexy. Ty dragged his tongue along my slit, and I couldn't help but try shifting closer to him. Ty's mouth wreaked havoc on my senses as he brought me to dizzying heights. When his tongue flicked my clit, I saw stars. He sucked the bud into his mouth, and I cried out as I thrust against his lips. I wanted more! So much more.

I could feel my body tightening and reaching for something I'd never experienced before. I'd read about orgasms, but I'd never actually had one. His touch burned me as his palms pressed my thighs outward, opening me more to his questing tongue and lips. He sucked, licked, and tormented me until I thought I would cry and scream from both frustration and pleasure. When I didn't think I could take another moment of it, he flicked my clit hard with his tongue and everything went hot and bright. I couldn't catch my breath as I screamed out my release, my body bowing as he relentlessly teased my clit. Stars exploded behind my eyelids as my body slowly relaxed, and I came back down to earth.

Ty kissed his way up my body, and I felt his cock

brush against my pussy. I trembled, knowing what he wanted, and was more than ready to give it to him. But I wanted something else first. I wanted to please him the way he'd pleased me. It only seemed fair, and I was more than a little curious. This might be my first time, but I also knew it might be my only time for a while, and I wanted to make the best of it.

"Not yet," I said softly.

He pulled away, looking pained. "You want to stop?"

I licked my lips. "No, I want to taste you. The way you tasted me."

Heat blazed in his gaze as he helped me off the bed. I fell to my knees in front of him, looking up to see if this was what he wanted. He tangled his fingers in my hair and urged me closer. The musky scent of him hit my nose and my mouth watered. I wrapped my hand around the base of his cock, surprised at how soft the skin felt compared to the hardness of his shaft. My tongue flicked out and gathered the drop of pre-cum that had been on his tip. He tasted salty, but not bad.

Ty groaned as I fitted my lips around the head of his cock and slowly took him into my mouth. I remembered reading that the area just under the head was sensitive, and I flicked it with my tongue. His hold on my hair tightened, and I could feel his control starting to snap. I wasn't sure what he wanted me to do, so I explored and savored him as much as I could. I couldn't fit his entire cock in my mouth, but I used my hand to make up the difference.

"Josie." My name sounded like a prayer on his lips. "I want to fuck that luscious mouth of yours."

I pulled away long enough to look up at him. "Then do it."

"You don't know what you're asking."

"Yes, I do." I flicked the head of his cock with my tongue. "You want to fuck my mouth, then do it. Just try not to choke me."

I opened my mouth and took him inside again, letting him have control. He fucked my mouth with slow, shallow thrusts that soon turned to deeper, harder strokes. My jaw ached, but I loved the feel and taste of him in my mouth.

"That's it, baby. Take it all. You like it when I fuck your mouth, don't you?"

I hummed my approval.

"Christ! You feel so fucking fantastic. Suck it, baby. Suck down every fucking drop."

His dirty words just turned me on even more, and I clenched my thighs together. I could feel his body tensing and knew he was close to coming. There was no warning before he erupted in my mouth. I swallowed, trying to take every drop of what he gave me, and when he finished, he released me.

I licked my lips and rose to my feet, marveling at the fact he was still hard. I'd always thought men went soft after they came, but that didn't seem to be true for Ty. He growled softly before claiming my lips in a searing kiss that I felt all the way to my toes. He urged me back onto the bed and covered my body with his. I knew what was coming next, and I was more than ready for it. My body hummed with anticipation, and I knew I was more than wet enough to take him.

"I'm going to ask one last time. Are you sure this is what you want?"

"I'm sure. I want you to be the one, Ty. I trust you."

He retrieved a condom from the bedside table, and I watched as he rolled it on. I'd never seen one up close before, and it squeezed tight over his cock. I wondered if it was painful. If I'd been on birth control, I might have told him he didn't need one. I wanted there to be no barriers between us, but I knew that wasn't very smart.

He kissed me again as his fingers slid against my slippery pussy. He eased a finger inside of me. It wasn't unpleasant, but it felt odd. As he pumped in and out of me, my body began to loosen as pleasure zinged through me. He added another finger and slowly fucked me with them. It felt incredible, and I couldn't wait to have him inside of me. Any pain I might feel would be well worth it.

"Now, Ty."

He didn't need any further urging. He lined up his cock with my pussy and slowly pressed into me. My breath caught and held at the intrusion. It was a tight fit and hurt like hell as my inner walls burned and ached as he stretched me. It felt like it was taking forever and I wondered when the pleasure would come back.

"This part is going to hurt more," he warned before surging forward.

I cried out in shock and pain and he froze, holding still inside of me. I don't know how long we stayed like that, but the pain began to fade and soon I wanted him to move again. His thrusts were slow as if he were afraid he would break me. My body began to warm, and the pleasure returned, even more intense than before. I could tell he was holding back, and I wanted him to let loose, to give me everything he had.

"More, Ty."

He nipped my neck as he thrust into me hard, deeper. My legs wrapped around his waist as he pounded into me. Sweat coated our skin, and I felt his muscles bunch and flex with every move. I'd never felt so connected to anyone before, had never felt so complete.

Everything felt like it was spiraling out of control and as he thrust harder and deeper, I cried out my second release, holding onto to him tight. Ty gave a hoarse cry as he stilled inside of me, our hips pressed together. He gave me another kiss as he pulled away, withdrawing from my body. I missed him the moment he was gone. His muffled curse had me opening my eyes to see what was wrong.

"It broke." He was staring at his cock.

"What broke?" Surely he didn't mean I'd broken his dick.

"The condom, Josie. The fucking condom broke."

"Oh." I blinked at him. "It probably takes more than one time to get pregnant, right? I mean, couples try all the time for months on end before having a baby."

He stormed into the bathroom and returned a moment later without the condom and with a hot rag in his hand. I winced as he cleaned me, pressing the hot cloth to my sensitive pussy. Having never been intimate with someone before, I wasn't sure what came next. Was it time for me to go? Would he want to cuddle? Since the condom had broken and he didn't look too pleased, I was going to go with option one. I pushed myself up and reached for my clothes, but he took them from me, tossing them aside.

"I'm not going to fuck you and throw you out of my house," he said. "Did you think you'd overstayed your welcome?"

"Something like that. You seemed angry, so I thought it was best if I left."

He sighed and shook his head, kneeling in front of me. "Josie, I'm not mad at you. I'm upset the condom broke because I've never had that happen before. But that doesn't mean it's your fault or that I hold it against you. If you want to stay a little longer, I'm okay with that. It was your first time, and I'm not about to treat you like some whore who needs to get the fuck out of my bed right afterward."

I scooted over and waited for him to climb back into bed, then I curled against his side and rested my head on his shoulder. It was nice, cuddling with him, and it was something I could easily get used to. Ty was the kind of man I'd always wanted, and even though I knew this was a one-time deal it was nice that he was mine even for a little while. Today would have to be a memory that would hold me for a while. I wasn't sure when my parents planned to spring Falks on me again, but thanks to Ty, the good reverend would no longer want me. I only hoped this didn't come back to bite me in the ass.

Chapter Three

Ty

It had been weeks since my afternoon with Josie and fuck if I could get her out of my head. I'd had a date scheduled for the next day, but the woman had seemed vapid and I'd ditched her as fast as I could. Since then, I hadn't been tempted by so much as one female. Except Josie. I had seen her around town a few times, but she'd always been looking the other way, or with her parents. If possible she looked thinner, and I worried about her health. There were circles under her eyes, and I knew she wasn't sleeping. I wondered if that was because of me and what we'd done, or if her parents were still pushing the marriage to Reverend Falks.

It was a Wednesday night, and Josie was probably at church with her family. I sat at the counter in the Southern Fried Café waiting on my dinner. I'd gotten off a shift a half hour before, but I was too damn hungry to go home and change before eating. The loaded burger that Estelle placed in front of me was well worth a little discomfort. My damn belt weighed a ton, but all that faded away at the thought of food. Damn burger smelled incredible, and my stomach growled.

"It's a shame if you ask me," an old-timer down the counter said. "Good girl like that. Don't know what her parents are thinking."

The hairs on my nape prickled.

"I'm sorry, but who's a good girl?" I asked, dreading his answer.

"Josie Wright. Her parents threw her out from what I heard. She's been living in her car the last few days. Makes me question just how Christian her folks could be to do something like that."

"Oh, they had a good reason," Charlotte Weathers said from across the room. "Can't say why, doctor-patient confidentiality and all that, but she was in to see Doc Simms the other day and her mama just about went through the roof."

Was Josie sick? And her parents had thrown her out?

"Where's she parking her car?" I asked.

"Out at Grovener Park. She parks under the shade tree out that way, or at least that's where I've seen her the past two nights," the old-timer said.

"Estelle, would you please make my dinner to-go, and get me a second one as well?" I asked.

The waitress smiled and nodded, taking my plate to the back. About ten minutes later, she had two to-go containers for me, and I was out the door. I wanted to flip on my lights and barrel through town to get to Josie, but I didn't want to get my ass chewed by the chief. When I pulled into the parking lot of the park, that bright red Beetle was hard to miss. Josie had the seat tilted back, and it looked like she was already asleep.

I got out of my cruiser and tapped on her window. She bolted upright, her eyes wide, and I felt like an ass for scaring the shit out of her. Josie rolled down her window and stared up at me.

"Am I in trouble for parking here?"

"You're in trouble all right. Why the hell didn't you come to me when your parents threw you out?"

Tears gathered in her eyes, and she started sobbing. With a curse, I jerked open her door and pulled her into my arms, her ass resting across my bent legs. Her arms curled around my neck, and she held on tight like she was afraid I would let her go. Fat chance of that. She was all I'd thought about for weeks, and now that she was back in my arms, I wasn't going to let her go again.

"Are you okay to drive?" I asked. "Or do you want to come back for your car?"

"I can drive." She sniffled and wiped her eyes.

"Follow me home. I have some dinner for you when you get there. I picked up some burgers at Southern Fried before I came here. I could tan your ass for not telling me they'd thrown you out. Why the hell didn't you come to me, Josie?"

"I didn't think you'd want us," she said softly.

"Us?" I looked into her car but didn't see anyone else in there.

"Me and…" She hiccupped. "Our baby."

"Our…" My gaze dropped to her flat stomach. "Are you saying you're pregnant?"

She nodded.

Fuck me.

"Follow me home and we'll talk about this some more."

I let her get back into her car and then I got into my cruiser and headed for home, checking the rearview every few minutes to make sure she was still back there. My mind was reeling with her news. She was pregnant? Fuck. I'd never really thought about being a dad before, but it seemed it would happen whether I was ready or not. Christ! A kid? It was one thing to think about Josie every waking moment, but another to raise a kid with her. What the fuck did I know about raising kids? Jesus, would she expect me to marry her?

Oddly, the thought of putting a ring on Josie's finger didn't freak me the fuck out like I'd thought it would. Knowing she was home every night, waiting for me, was actually a pretty nice idea. I'd stayed away from commitment as long as I could, not dating anyone more than once or twice, but Josie deserved more from me. She was having my baby for fuck's sake.

When I pulled into my driveway, a sigh of relief left me when I saw her pull up to the curb out front. There was plenty of room in the driveway for both cars, which made me think she didn't intend to stay very long. We'd see about that. No way in hell was the mother of my kid going to sleep in her car every night at the park. Our town might be small and low on crime, but that didn't mean bad things didn't happen. If we were completely crime free, I wouldn't have had a damn job.

Josie followed me up to the front door and I let her in, shutting off the alarm. I'd have to make sure I gave her a key and the alarm code so she could come and go as she pleased. Whether she realized it or not, this was her home now too. I carried our food into the kitchen and got down two plates. I wasn't about to make her eat out of a Styrofoam carton.

She'd made herself at home in the living room, and I handed her a plate and a bottle of water. I wasn't sure if pregnant women were supposed to drink soda, but I damn sure planned to look it up first chance I got. Whatever she needed, I'd make sure she had it.

"I'm going to grab a shower and change, and then I'll eat something. After that, we're going to talk." I reached out and lifted her chin to make sure she was looking at me. "You're not alone, Josie."

She blinked tears from her eyes and nodded.

I left her to eat her meal, and I took the fastest damn shower ever before throwing on some athletic pants. I grabbed my food out of the kitchen and sat beside her on the couch to devour my meal. Despite her shocking news, my appetite was still raging, and my stomach demanded to be fed. By the time we were both done, she looked worn the fuck out. Without a word, I picked her up and carried her to my bedroom, where I slipped off her shoes and helped her strip down to her panties. I handed her one of my T-shirts and helped her to bed.

"Sleep as long as you want," I told her. "I'll come to bed in a little while, but I expect you to still be here come morning. Understood?"

"Thank you, Ty."

"You don't have to thank me, Josie. I'm just glad someone told me what was going on. I still want to spank that ass of yours for not coming to me right away."

Her cheeks warmed, and I wondered if she wasn't a little turned on by the idea. Definitely something to explore later.

I brushed a kiss against her cheek and left her to get some rest. I grabbed my laptop and settled onto the couch to do a little research on pregnancy. If there was something in particular Josie needed, I wanted to make sure she had it. We hadn't really talked about her pregnancy or the baby, so I didn't know if she was having cravings or nausea. The blogs I read said a lot of women experienced morning sickness during their first trimester. Not that I'd had a fucking clue what a trimester was before I looked it up.

By the time I'd finished my research, I felt a little better prepared for our talk in the morning. Before I went to bed, I called the police department and let them know I wouldn't be in for my shift tomorrow. It seemed word was already spreading around town that Josie had followed me home and dispatch asked if she was okay. I assured them she was going to be fine and hung up before they could ask any more questions. Until Josie and I talked, I didn't want anyone speculating on why she was here.

My eyes burned from staring at the computer screen. I made sure the alarm by the front door was set before I went to the bedroom. Josie was still curled on her side so I slid into bed next to her, wrapping an arm around her waist and pulling her back against my chest. It was the first time I'd ever actually *slept* with a woman, and it seemed right that the woman was Josie.

Despite how tired I felt, it was a while before I fell asleep. Even though I didn't have an alarm set for the next day, I still woke when the sun rose. Force of habit. Josie was snuggled against me, and I didn't want to wake her. I knew my kitchen had limited options for breakfast, but I wasn't sure if she'd feel like going out to eat either. Easing out from under her, I threw on a T-shirt and shoes and quietly left the house.

The diner wasn't busy this time of the morning, and it didn't take long to get two breakfast specials to go. If the knowing smirk from the waitress was any indication, everyone already knew who the second meal was for. I just hoped they didn't know why Josie was staying with me, not until I'd figured out how we were going to handle things. The fact she was pregnant with my kid meant she was my responsibility, whether she saw things that way or not. The question was just how committed did we want to be? Having a baby was one thing, but did it mean she'd want to marry me?

The jewelry store was closed this time of the morning, but the pawn shop was just opening up. On impulse, I pulled into the lot and ran inside. Rob, the owner, smiled when he saw me hurry through the doors. It wasn't often we had a chance to meet when I was out of uniform unless it was at the local bar.

"What can I do for you this morning, Ty? Or is it Officer Daniels and this is a new uniform requirement?"

"Smart ass."

He grinned.

"I need a ring, and I need you to keep quiet about it."

His eyebrows shot up. "An engagement ring?"

"You do have those, right?"

"A few." He motioned for me to follow him over to a glass countertop. The rings were on display on the shelf below, ranging from diamonds so small you could barely see them to a diamond so large I knew it would break the bank even in a pawn shop.

"I only have about a hundred dollars in my wallet. I don't suppose you have anything for that amount? I wasn't really prepared for something like this." I stared at the rings, hoping I could present Josie with something other than the tiniest diamond in the bunch.

Rob reached into the cabinet and pulled out a ring that wasn't a diamond solitaire, but a sapphire with diamond chips on either side. It was set in a silver band and looked elegant, even though the stones were on the small side.

"This is a platinum band, so it's good quality. I can let you have it for one hundred, even though I'm asking two hundred for it. I'll give you the thin blue line special."

"Are you sure? I don't want to screw up your profit on the ring."

"It's for Josie, isn't it?"

"Yeah."

"Then I'm sure."

I handed over the money, and he gave me the

ring in a small black velvet box. I snapped the lid shut and shoved it into my pants pocket. Rob wrote up a receipt, and I shoved it in my wallet before heading back out to my car. The food was still hot, and I rushed home so Josie could eat before it got cold. I was glad I'd made my extra stop, though. The more I thought about asking her to marry me, the more it seemed like the right thing to do. I liked to think if we'd had a chance at a normal relationship that things would have progressed to that point naturally.

Josie was awake and sitting on the couch when I walked in, the TV on low. There was a bottle of water on the table in front of her, and I cursed myself for not thinking about getting some juice for her while I was out. If she was going to move in, I would definitely need to stock the kitchen with mama-to-be type food and drinks. She smiled, relief flooding her eyes as I walked through the door with the food containers in my hand.

"How long have you been awake?" I asked.

"Not long. I thought maybe you'd gone to work."

"No, but I do need to return the cruiser sometime tonight. I took today off and I'm scheduled to be off the next two days, so I need to pick up my personal vehicle. I only keep the cruiser on nights when I might get called in." I held up the containers. "Are you hungry? I have eggs, bacon, sausage, and toast."

Her stomach growled, and I smiled.

"Just let me put everything on plates and I'll be back."

"No." She held out a hand. "I can eat out of the container. Just bring me a fork."

I went to the kitchen and grabbed forks for both of us and then settled on the couch beside her. We ate in silence with her watching the TV, even though she seemed more interested in her food than what was on. It made me wonder just how often she'd gotten to eat since her parents threw her out. If she didn't have a job, it wasn't likely she'd had much cash on her at the time, if any.

When we were finished, I threw the containers away and put the forks in the sink before returning to Josie. She seemed nervous, and I couldn't blame her. She'd been through a lot in the last few days, but I aimed to see that she was taken care of from this point on, as much as she would allow. Josie had been dependent on her parents her entire life, and from what little I knew about her, I knew that wasn't the type of woman she wanted to be. If she wanted to work, to have her independence, then I didn't have a problem with that. But if she wanted to be a stay-at-home mom, I would be okay with that too. I might not be rich, but I made enough that we could live comfortably as long as we didn't go on crazy buying sprees.

"You said last night that you're pregnant," I said.

She nodded.

"Why didn't you come tell me?"

"I didn't think you'd want to know. It was just the one time, and I knew you were doing me a favor. It's not like we were dating. I don't expect for you to swoop in like some white knight and take care of me, Ty. I'll figure things out."

"Josie..." I reached out and took her hand. "We might not have planned this, but that's still my baby you're carrying and I have every right to be a part of his or her life. It also means that I'm going to take care of you. I know you want to stand on your own two feet and I'm fine with that, but right now you need some help. You need a place to stay at the very least, and that place is going to be here."

"Is this where you go all caveman on me and throw me over your shoulder, carrying me off to the bedroom?"

I smiled. "It's not a bad idea. I'd be lying if I said I hadn't thought about you every damn day since our afternoon together. I've looked for you around town, but you never noticed me. Or if you did, you did a damn fine job of pretending otherwise. I'm not trying to dictate your life, but I do want an active role in my son or daughter's life."

She stared at our joined hands, and I wondered what she was thinking. The ring was burning in my pocket, begging to be taken out, but I knew if I did that right now it would blow up in my face. She wasn't ready for me to propose, and she might never be ready for that step. I wanted her to be mine, even if it had taken an unplanned pregnancy to make me see that. I just wasn't sure that Josie would appreciate my sudden devotion. I had no intention of sleeping with other women or even looking twice at them. Now that I knew we were going to be a family, I had a reason to reach out and grab what I wanted.

"You aren't mad?" she asked.

"Why would I be mad? It's not like you trapped me. The condom broke, which isn't my fault or yours. It's not like you sleep around and you're trying to pawn someone else's kid off on me." I squeezed her hand. "It may not have been intentional, but we're having a baby whether we're ready or not. You don't have a place to live right now, and I think we get along reasonably well. Will you please consider living here? And not as a roommate."

"This isn't who you are, is it? The soft, caring

man. I've seen you with those other women, and you've always been dominant and demanding. I've heard the talk around town, so I knew what I was signing up for when I agreed to come to your house. But that's not the side I've seen, and it's left me wondering which is the real Ty Daniels."

"Can't I be both?"

She shook her head. "I think you've been treating me differently because I was a virgin and you were worried you'd scare me, or lose control. But in the end, isn't that exactly what you've done? You've given all the control to me, and that's not who you are, Ty. I want you to be the real you when you're around me. I'm a big girl, and I can handle it."

Fuck me. She was giving me permission to be myself, and hell if she wasn't right. I'd been holding back with her. At first, it was because she was a virgin, but now I knew there was a baby growing inside of her, and I was scared as hell I'd do something to hurt one or both of them. What kind of asshole would I be if I handcuffed the mother of my child to my bed?

"I don't think you can handle the real me." I released her hand and stood up, pacing the small space. When I neared Josie again, she dropped to her knees and gripped my hips with her hands.

"Then let me prove to you that I can."

"You shouldn't be on your knees right now."

"Why not?"

I growled.

"Does it make you want to do dirty things to me?" she asked with a smile. "Does it make you want to strip me naked and fuck my mouth like you did that afternoon?"

"Yes."

"Then do it."

- 171 -

"Josie, I'm not playing."

"I never said this was a game. You want me, and I want you. The only problem is that you're scared to let loose, and I'm telling you it's okay. Take what you want from me, Ty. I'm yours to do with as you please."

Holy shit! Did she have any idea how fucking hot that was? My dick was trying to break free of my pants, and fuck if I didn't want to take her up on her offer. She wanted the real me? Maybe it was time I showed her who that was.

"Take off your clothes, Josie. New rule. No clothes in the house unless I tell you to put something on. When we're alone, when you walk in the door you strip naked."

I watched her eyes dilate as she swiped her tongue across her lower lip. It seemed my Josie liked that idea. A lot.

She quickly stripped out of her clothes and sank back to her knees in front of me, waiting for my next command. There were so many things I wanted to do to her, and I fully intended to explore each and every one at some point, but right now she was going to suck me dry.

"Take out of my cock."

She reached up and pulled my pants down to my hips, and my cock sprang free. She licked her lips again, anticipating my next demand. Pre-cum dripped from the tip, but fuck if I was going to blow my load before I got between those sweet lips.

"Open."

Her jaw dropped and I thrust my cock between her lips. She greedily sucked and licked at my shaft as I fucked her mouth with shallow thrusts. I knew I was too big for her to take the whole thing, and I sure as hell didn't want to choke her. *Fuck*! She felt incredible.

My hand knotted in her hair as I tilted her head back a little so I could go a bit deeper.

"You like that, don't you? Like being treated like a good little whore?"

She hummed around my dick, and my balls drew up.

"Mmm. Do that again, baby."

She made her humming sound again, and I nearly lost it. I fucked her mouth faster, wanting to come. I was so damn close.

"Reach up and play with my balls."

Her small, soft hand closed around my balls, and I nearly came right then. She rolled them between her fingers and when she gave them a little squeeze, I exploded, shooting cum down the back of her throat. I pulled out before I was completely empty and painted her lips with my cum. When she licked it off, I was almost instantly hard again.

She had been a virgin when I fucked her a few weeks ago, but damn if she wasn't acting like a pro. I had no idea what she'd been up to since we'd been apart, but I was wondering if a little porn-watching hadn't been part of her spare time. Even more, I wanted to know if she'd gotten herself off while she'd been back home.

"Did you play with yourself after you went home that day? Have you gotten yourself off?" I asked. I wondered if she'd become a little more daring after our time together.

Her cheeks flushed, and she nodded.

"And what were you thinking about when you did that?"

"You. I remembered the things we'd done together, and it made me so wet." Her thighs clenched. "I'm wet now."

"Do you need a good fucking, sweet Josie?"

She nodded eagerly.

"Get on the couch and wait for me."

I didn't hang around to see if she complied. I had a stash of new toys in the bedroom, things I'd bought with Josie in mind even though I hadn't been certain I'd ever have her in my bed again. I'd gotten off a lot just thinking about using them on her. I opened a small vibrator and made sure I put in batteries, then I grabbed some lube and a butt plug. She'd given me her virgin pussy, and now she was going to give me her virgin ass. I was so fucking hard just thinking about it.

I'd passed some long hours in the cruiser, thinking about bending her over the hood of my car and fucking her ass good and deep. I wanted to coat every inch of her in my cum, marking her as mine. Because whether she knew it or not, she was mine now. It was just a matter of time before I claimed her officially. The ring in my pocket felt heavy. I pulled it out and shoved it into a dresser drawer. Now wasn't the time.

In the living room, she was curled up on the couch, her knees folded under her. Her eyes widened when she saw what I was carrying, but she didn't utter a word of protest. So, she was either intrigued, or just didn't want to disappoint me. I was really hoping for the first one.

"I've painted those luscious lips of yours with my cum. Now I'm going to bathe your pussy and your ass with it. If you're going to protest, now is the time."

She shook her head and watched me as I knelt in front of her. I pulled her legs from under her and spread them wide. Her pussy was so pink and inviting, just begging to be fucked. I leaned forward and licked her slit, gathering her essence on my tongue. Pulling her closer, until her ass nearly hung off the edge of the couch, I set to work pleasing her. I fucked her with my mouth until she was on the verge of coming, her little clit so hard that I could feel the blood pulsing inside.

"Does my Josie want to come?" I asked.

"Yes, please."

"I'm going to make you come, and then I'm going to fill your ass with the butt plug while I fuck you good and hard. You want that, don't you, Josie?"

"Yes." She whimpered. "Please, Ty. I need you."

I pulled out the vibrator and turned it on high, placing it against her clit. She nearly screamed as she orgasmed right away, her body bowing off the couch. I didn't let up, knowing she had more than one orgasm to give me. As I tormented her clit with the toy, I fucked her with my fingers. My dick ached to be inside of her, and there was a steady stream of pre-cum puddling on my wood floor.

I watched as her ass clenched on her next orgasm, and it made me even more determined to take her there. I was going to ride her ass long and hard tonight. When I thought she'd had enough, I helped her roll over onto her knees, and I used a liberal amount of lube to prep her ass. I teased her with my finger until I felt her relax, then I gently pushed inside, just up to the first knuckle. I wanted her in the worst way, but I was going to take my time and do this right. Sweat was coating my skin by the time I'd worked two fingers into her ass and was ready to insert the butt plug.

I eased the toy inside of her, making sure she wasn't in any pain. By the time it was fully inserted, she was moaning and pressing back, asking for more. I had no doubt that she was going to give me a wild ride when it came time to switch the toy for my dick.

"What does my Josie want now?" I asked, flicking the butt plug.

"I want you, Ty. I want you to fuck me."

I teased her slit. "You want my dick to fill up this pretty pussy?"

"Please."

That *please* was the sweetest thing I'd ever heard. I helped her readjust so that I could climb onto the couch behind her. As my cock sank into her wet heat, I reached for the vibrator and switched it on again. Balls deep inside of her, I tormented her little clit with the vibrator until she was screaming and thrashing beneath me. My little Josie was something of a wildcat, and fuck if that didn't make me even harder.

I pumped into her with deep, long strokes, wanting to feel every inch of her. It wasn't long before she was pushing back against every thrust and whimpering for more. I pounded into her, taking her fast and hard, until both of us cried out our releases. I shot load after load of cum into that sweet pussy, marking her as mine. When I pulled out, it dripped down her thighs, and I couldn't help but smile in satisfaction. I'd never gone bare with a woman before, but fuck me if it wasn't the biggest high.

"I don't think my legs work," she mumbled into the cushions.

"Oh, I'm not done with you yet."

She turned her head and cracked an eye open to peer up at me. "If we fuck like rabbits all day long, I won't be able to walk tomorrow."

Chapter Four

Josie

The plug in my ass was a reminder of things to come. Once we'd caught our breath we'd showered, then Ty had told me to get dressed. Even though I'd already seen Doc Simms, he insisted on taking me back and hearing everything for himself. This time we took his personal vehicle. It seemed he was going to be an attentive father, and it made me think he was serious about being in this for the long haul. I only hoped Doc didn't ask me to strip, or things were going to get a little embarrassing.

"Josie, Doc said he'd like to do an ultrasound this time, to get a better idea of how far along you are." The nurse smiled. "I know your mom rushed you out of here last time."

"I know exactly how far along I am. I've only had sex one time in my entire life."

The nurse's eyes widened and cut toward Ty, a knowing grin on her lips. I sure as hell hoped Ty *was* in this for the long haul because the town gossip mill was about to start churning. Not that I was expecting a wedding or anything, but I was glad he wanted to be a part of his child's life. As for me, I had no doubt I'd eventually land on my feet. I just needed a little more time to figure things out. I'd wanted to go to college, but my parents had considered it a waste of time.

Ty helped me onto the table, the paper crinkling under my ass. I'd thought he would take a seat across the room but he stood beside me, his hand braced on my thigh. It was sweet, the way he watched over me, but I didn't want to get used to it. Sooner or later I'd have to face the fact it was time to move on. Everyone around town knew about Ty and his stance on relationships. He was a fuck 'em and leave 'em kind of guy, and I seriously doubted that a romp between the sheets with a virgin had changed him. It wasn't like I had a magic pussy or anything. He'd probably had better, even if he had seemed to enjoy himself both times.

Ty rubbed between my eyes. "You're frowning," he said. "If you don't want the ultrasound, we won't get one. I don't know anything about having a baby, but it's probably too soon to see much of anything anyway."

"I'm sure my parents' insurance will cover it if they haven't pulled me already. I just..." I sighed. Now was not the time to discuss where this thing between us was going, if anywhere.

The door opened, and Doc Simms walked in, a jovial smile on his face.

"I'm surprised to see you back so soon, Josie. I take it now that you've had time to think things over you're a little more excited about the baby?" he asked.

"It wasn't so much a lack of excitement before as it was a shock that I was pregnant. My mother's screeching didn't help matters any."

He hummed an agreement. "Well, why don't you lie back and we'll take a look at your baby? My nurse tells me that you know the date of conception, but I'd still like to take a peek and make sure everything looks good."

I swung my legs onto the table and leaned back, pulling my shirt up to expose my stomach. Ty moved closer and reached for my hand. I gripped it tight as Doc squirted a cold gel on my stomach and then started moving the wand around. There was a loud noise that filled the room as the grainy images appeared on the screen. I had no idea what I was looking for and hoped Doc would point out the baby. For all I knew, it looked like an alien right now.

He pressed down harder as he slid the wand around my stomach and then he stopped moving and pushed some buttons on the machine. A moment later, he handed Ty a black and white picture.

"Congratulations, Daddy. You now have your first picture of your son or daughter. According to your paperwork Josie, you're about six weeks along right now. At the five month mark, we'll do another ultrasound, and you should be able to find out what you're having if the little tadpole decides to cooperate. Do the two of you have any questions for me?"

"I read that caffeine isn't good for the baby," Ty said. "Is it still okay for her to have some coffee and soda? Or does she need to cut it out completely?"

Doc folded his arms. "I don't see the harm in one cup of coffee and maybe one or two sodas a day, but try to limit caffeine intake as much as you can. If possible, only drink one or the other. You should really focus on milk and juice to get the vitamins and nutrients you need. Did you get your prescription filled for the prenatal vitamins?"

I shook my head. "Mom tore it up."

Doc sighed. "I'll write you another one. Make sure you get it filled this time. You should also eat well-balanced meals and swap any sugary snacks for things like fruit or yogurt. You're going to notice a dip in your energy levels before it shoots back up and you go into nesting mode."

"Nesting mode?" I asked.

Doc smiled at Ty. "If your house isn't clean now, it will be later. I've found that most expecting mothers want the house to be perfect before they bring home their babies, even if that means hand-washing the baseboards."

Ty's eyebrows rose. "I read something about that last night, but I didn't realize it was a real thing."

"Oh yeah. Just don't let her overdo it."

Ty cleared his throat. "What about... intimacy?"

Doc chuckled. "As long as she's up for it and no pregnancy issues pop up in the future, then you can have a relatively normal sex life until the last few weeks of her pregnancy. I'd like you to stop the closer we get to her due date because sperm can cause the cervix to thin and orgasms can cause contractions. Don't want the little one showing up too soon."

My cheeks burned, but I was glad Ty had asked. If he intended to continue our relationship, I was certain that sex would be part of it. If last night was any indication, keeping our hands off each other would be difficult. The plug in my ass reminded me that he wasn't finished with me yet. If he wanted me as much as I wanted him, then we'd barely clear the front door before the clothes would start flying. I was twenty-one and had never felt so much as a twinge of desire before Ty, and now I felt like a sex-starved rabbit. All I wanted to do was fuck Ty in every way imaginable.

Doc spoke with Ty for a few more minutes about some concerns he had and then we were on our way. My stomach rumbled, and a glance at the clock showed it was nearly noon. We'd been at my appointment longer than I'd thought. Ty reached over and rubbed my belly.

"Guess we better feed the little bean. Are you hungry for anything in particular? I read that pregnant women have cravings."

It seemed he'd done a lot of research while I was sleeping last night and it warmed my heart, giving me hope that things might work out. I still didn't kid myself into believing I could have it all, but at least I knew he'd be an attentive father for our child. A lot of single moms didn't even have that much. We could work out a schedule that worked well for him so that he could spend as much time with the baby as he wanted. Assuming I'd figured out what the hell I was doing with my life and I wasn't still dependent on him for survival. It was really going to suck if I had this baby before I figured things out. At this point, any job would be better than no job, but who was going to hire a pregnant woman?

"Josie?"

I snapped my gaze his way and remembered that he'd asked me a question.

"Oh. Food. Um, anything is fine. Except for seafood. Maybe some pasta?"

"Little Italy, then."

My stomach rumbled again, this time in approval. I'd eaten there several times with my family, but I'd never gone there -- or anywhere -- on a date before. Was this a date? No, this was just Ty feeding the mother of his unborn child. I didn't need to romanticize it. But we really did need to have a conversation about what his expectations were. I might have a long way to go with this pregnancy, but I didn't want the uncertainty of my future, of my child's future, hanging over my head the entire time.

Ty found a spot near the front door and escorted me inside, his hand at the small of my back. I'd hoped we were getting our food to go so we could pick up where we'd left off at home, but he asked for a table. It seemed he was intent on driving me insane. Every time I moved, every time I sat, the plug in my ass sent off little shockwaves. By the time he finally got around to fucking me, I'd probably come just from looking at his dick.

My cheeks burned at my thoughts. I'd never been wanton before or felt so naughty. I'd definitely never thought dirty thoughts. Even when I'd had a bit of a crush on Ty, I'd never thought much past kissing and being held. I might have read hundreds of romance books, but since I'd never actually had sex, I'd not really had a clue how those sensations would feel when the writer described something. Now I knew firsthand how amazing sex was, and I wanted more of it.

The waitress who came to take our order kept smiling and batting her eyes at Ty. If he'd given her even the slightest hint of a smile or flirted back, I might have stabbed him with my butter knife. I had no clue where these out of control emotions were coming from, but I hoped I could get a grip on them soon. It was one thing to want to climb my baby-daddy like a tree and have wild monkey sex, but it was another to want to bare my teeth and claim him as mine. I had a feeling Ty wouldn't appreciate that much.

Even when I placed my drink order, the stupid woman didn't even look at me.

"Does that happen often?" I asked as she walked away.

"What? Wait staff asking to take my order?"

"No, getting eye-fucked by anything in a skirt."

His lips twitched and amusement lit his eyes. "Usually, it's the uniform that does it. But yes, women tend to throw themselves at me."

I wasn't happy with that bit of news, but I had to stifle my current feelings and lock them away. We might be having a baby, but Ty was very much still single and could do as he pleased.

"I wouldn't have stopped you if you'd wanted her number." My hands fidgeted in my lap as my brain screamed *lie*. As it was, I'd wanted to rip out her eyes for looking at him too long. I had no doubt she'd been picturing him naked -- in bed, no doubt.

His eyes darkened, and his mouth firmed into a thin line. "Is that what you think of me? Do you honestly think I'd pick up another woman while I'm having a meal with the mother of my child?"

"Ty." I sighed. "That's all I am. The mother of your child. We aren't boyfriend and girlfriend. I have no claim on you. I'm sure sharing a house will cramp your style a bit, but it's not like I moved in last night and demanded your fidelity."

"Maybe you didn't have to demand it, and it was freely given." He nearly growled at me. "I'm not a complete asshole, Josie. I would never disrespect you that way. No, we may not have labeled whatever this is between us, but it sure as fuck is something. I'm not going to screw you over."

I smiled faintly. "You're just going to screw me?"

His anger faded as he smiled. "Definitely. Every chance I get."

The waitress brought our food, attempting to flirt with Ty once more. He still didn't pay her much attention other than to thank her. His eyes never left mine. Maybe I wasn't the only one feeling a little possessive. Perhaps he really did want me as much as I wanted him, and for now, that was enough.

We finished eating, and Ty paid the bill before ushering me back to the car. He locked the doors before starting the engine and turned my way, his gaze burning bright. I was trapped for a moment, unable to breathe or dare to look away.

"I think little Josie needs to be punished for

thinking so little of me."

Oh God. My thighs clenched as my clit throbbed.

"Punished?"

"Push your pants and panties down to your thighs."

"But... the windows. Someone will see."

He smirked. "They're tinted, but maybe I want them to see how much I can make you squirm. Maybe I want them to know that I can make you beg."

With my cheeks burning, more from intrigue than embarrassment, I slid my pants and panties down to mid-thigh. Ty backed out of the space and as he headed toward the house, his hand dipped between my legs and teased my pussy. He slid his fingers up and down my slit before spreading me open and seeking out my clit. Rubbing it in small, slow circles, it wasn't long before he had me panting. My nipples hardened and pushed against the cups of my bra as I tried to spread my legs further apart.

His finger left my clit and dipped inside of me, fucking me slowly. I wanted more! I wanted his mouth on me, I wanted his dick inside of me, I wanted... I wanted everything. Through the haze of pleasure, I realized he was taking me past the town limits, and he pulled down a bumpy dirt road, stopping slightly within view of the highway. My heart raced as I wondered what Ty was going to do next. We were still out in the open, exposed, and fuck if that didn't seem to excite me even more.

"Take your pants and panties the rest of the way off and get out of the car, Josie."

My eyes widened. "Out of the..."

"Car. Yes, strip and get out of the damn car."

I did as he demanded -- ditching my pants, panties, and shoes -- and as I stepped out, I heard him open the glove compartment. I didn't see what he pulled out, but I stood uncertainly beside the car. He came around the side and closed my door before bending me over the hood. His lips pressed to my ear sent a shiver down my spine.

"I'm going to make sure you know that the only pussy I want to fuck is yours. I'm going to take you hard. I'm going to take you fast. And I'm going to take you deep. Then after my cum is dripping down your thighs, I'm going to fuck this tight little ass of yours."

"What if someone sees us?"

I felt him smile against my neck. "Then I guess they'll get a free show. You'd like that wouldn't you, my little wildcat? You'd like someone watching as I fucked you into a coma."

My nipples were so damn hard, and my clit was throbbing. It seemed I had a bit of exhibitionist in me. I felt his cock against my pussy, and then he thrust inside with one long stroke. I cried out as my toes curled. His thrusts were strong and demanding. Relentless. I reached between my legs and played with my clit. My fingers flew as he took me faster and harder. I didn't want him to come without me. I was close, so close, but he roared his release before I could orgasm. I felt his teeth on my shoulder.

"Not getting to come yet is part of your punishment, little wildcat. You're really going to like this part."

I felt him ease the plug from my ass and then something cool dribbled in the crack of my ass. He'd brought lube? I wasn't sure if I was turned on that he was so prepared, or a little jealous that he drove around with lube in his car so he could have a quickie whenever the mood struck.

His cock probed my tight hole, and I sucked in a

breath as the head pushed through. The toy had prepared me some, but he was so damn big in comparison. It burned, but it didn't exactly hurt. Ty took his time, working his length into me until he was finally balls deep.

"So full," I murmured.

And then he began to move. Fuck me! I'd never felt anything like it before, and I hoped like hell he'd want to do this again sometime. Every nerve in my body tingled and snapped to awareness as he started out with a slow, steady rhythm. It wasn't long before I was pushing back against him, wanting more.

"Don't baby me," I said. "I know you want to fuck me."

He growled. "You want me to take you like an animal? You want to unleash the beast inside?"

"I want *you*, Ty. All of you. If that means you fuck me like an animal, then do it."

His grip on my hips tightened as he stroked deeper, harder. As he pounded my ass, my clit tingled and throbbed. I reached for it, wanting to come this time. I was so wet and slick that my fingers slid easily against the bud, moving faster and harder until I was crying out my release. I felt my ass tighten on his cock and it seemed to be all Ty needed to push him over the edge. He came with a roar, pumping into me until every last drop was drained from his dick. I had no doubt I was going to be one hot mess by the time we got home.

I squeaked in surprise when he put the butt plug back in.

"You'll wear that until we get home. Your clothes remain off until we pull into the driveway. Understand?"

I nodded as he helped me into the car. He

tenderly buckled me in, kissing the top of my head, before he went around and slid behind the wheel of the car. I had no idea what to expect next from Ty, but whatever it was, I was going to look forward to every moment of it. The man was insatiable, and if all of his punishments were as mind blowing as this one, I might have to be bad more often.

Chapter Five

Ty

I played with Josie's pussy the entire way home, bringing her to the brink at least twice more, yet not giving her the satisfaction of coming. When we pulled into the driveway, I let her get dressed. Not that she was going to stay dressed for long, but the neighbors might complain if she walked naked from the car to the front door. Might be time to find a house with a garage. Then it wouldn't have mattered if she had on clothes when we got home.

I turned off the alarm as we stepped inside and before the door had shut all the way, I was divesting her of her clothes. She was abso-fucking-lutely gorgeous, and I planned to keep her naked as much as possible. My cum was leaking out of her ass around the plug and dripping down her thighs from her pussy. It made me want to beat my chest like a caveman, having marked my woman. She didn't seem to realize that was what she was, though. Not if her comments at the restaurant were truly how she felt. Josie hadn't realized it yet, but she'd pulled my man whore card. Now I was a dedicated man whore to just one woman, and I intended to fuck her every chance I got.

"I'm going to run you a bath and let you soak. You're going to be sore."

"Are you going to join me?"

I smiled. "If I join you, you'll be even sorer. No… this bath is just for you. When you're done, we can discuss what you'd like to do for the rest of the day. I need to run to the store for some supplies at some point, but you can stay here and rest while I do that."

I went to the bathroom and started the water.

When I hadn't been able to get Josie out of my head, I'd purchased a few feminine bath products in case she ever came over again. I added some bubbles to the water and set out the shower gel and shampoo I'd picked up for her. The doc had said to make sure the water wasn't too hot, but fuck if I knew what too hot was. I liked my showers so hot my skin almost melted off, but I decided somewhere between reasonably hot and lukewarm was a safe bet.

When the tub was full, I shut off the water and went to collect Josie. She was still standing by the couch and hadn't moved.

"Everything okay?" I asked, worried that maybe I'd hurt her.

"I'm kind of messy. I didn't want to ruin the furniture."

I smiled. "It's leather, wildcat. I'm pretty sure we can wash it off. Come on. Your bath is ready."

I took her by the hand and led her to the master bath. Before she got in, I eased the plug from her ass and playfully bit her right ass cheek. She squealed and jumped a little. I gave her ass a light smack before helping her over the edge of the tub. As she sank neck-deep into the water, I knelt beside the tub.

"I'll be in the bedroom watching TV. Call me if you need anything."

"Ty, you don't have to hover. I'm pregnant, not fragile."

"Humor me." I kissed her softly before leaving her to her bath.

While Josie soaked in the tub, I brainstormed an idea for a proposal. After her comments at the restaurant, I knew I needed to make things more official between us. Women liked romantic gestures, or so I'd been told, but fuck if I knew exactly what that was. So far, our relationship consisted of me fucking her every chance I got. I looked out the bedroom window and the roses blooming in the backyard gave me an idea.

I crept through the house so Josie wouldn't question what I was up to, and went out back to gather a few blooms off the bushes that had come with the house. How the hell I hadn't killed them yet baffled me, but they seemed hardy enough. I grabbed a red, a pink, and a white before going back inside. When I got to the bedroom, I changed the sheets to the black ones I seldom used. I'd never fucked a woman on the black sheets, and at that moment I vowed to get rid of every article of bedding I had that had any miles on it.

Josie hummed softly in the bathroom as I broke the roses apart and sprinkled the petals across the sheets. I had a few candles that I kept mostly for power outages, but I lit them around the room and cut as much of the sunlight as I could. This was romantic, right? Music would have made things better, but I'd managed to break my iPod's docking station the week before and hadn't replaced it yet.

I heard the splash of water and the sound of the tub draining. I raced across to the dresser and pulled out the ring box, then stuffed it under my pillow. I was just straightening when she sauntered into the room, a towel wrapped around her body and her hair lying damp against her skin. My heart kicked in my chest at how gorgeous she was. If this plan worked, then she'd officially be mine.

She smiled when she saw the setting.

"What's all this?" she asked.

"I thought you deserved a little romance."

"Does this mean you're going to fuck me again?"

"No." I shook my head. "This means I'm going to

make love to you, which is something I've never done before just for the record. Fucked like a wild animal, yes, but made love to someone? No." Her eyes looked a little misty, and I hoped it was a good sign. "I realized over the last few weeks that you were more than a one-night stand, Josie. I've thought about you a lot since that day, and I wanted you to know that you're special to me. You're not just another woman in a long line of women."

She smiled a little.

I walked around the bed and tugged her into my arms. After dropping her towel to the floor, I laid her on the bed and stripped out of my clothes. Covering her body with mine, I kissed her softly. I'd never been one for words or tenderness, but I was going to try for Josie's sake. She deserved all that and more.

When I pulled back, her lips were swollen and her eyes heavy-lidded. I'd never understood the phrase "drunk on her kiss" until that moment. Whatever I was feeling, it wasn't something I'd felt before. But under that euphoria was a big dose of nerves as I slid my hand under my pillow and retrieved the box. I kept it out of her view a moment longer.

"Josie, I have something I want to ask you." I popped open the box and showed her the ring. "I know we don't know each other very well, despite our current circumstances, but I want to change that. I want to know everything there is to know about you, and I'd like to spend the rest of my life trying to figure you out. Marry me?"

Tears had gathered in her eyes and she reverently touched the ring. "Ty, you don't have to marry me just because of the baby."

"I'm asking you to marry me because I want to spend the rest of my life with you, Josie. I can't promise you flowery words or that I'll remember to always tell you what you mean to me, but I do promise to take care of you in whatever way you need and to love our child and provide for him or her to the best of my ability."

She stared at the ring, and I wondered if I was about to be rejected, but she turned those tear-filled eyes my way and nodded. My heart nearly stopped before taking off at a gallop.

"Is that a yes?" I asked, needing to be certain.

"Yes." She laughed. "Yes, I'll marry you, Ty."

I kissed her hungrily before sliding the ring onto her finger. I threw the box halfway across the room before I devoted all of my attention to my future wife. Her body was my playground, and I was going to make her scream my name until she couldn't anymore. I kept my touch gentle as I explored her curves, my mouth tasting every inch I could reach.

I slid down her body and pushed her thighs wide with my shoulders. The lips of her pussy parted, and fuck if my cock didn't get even harder. The scent of her arousal was addicting, and I knew it was a scent I would never grow tired of, no matter how long we were together. I hoped when I was sixty I'd still want to pull off onto the side of the road to fuck her.

My lips closed over her clit, and I sucked the little bud until Josie's thighs were tightening on me. She tasted sweet, and I couldn't wait to gather her cream on my tongue. I licked, sucked, and savored every inch of her pussy. My little wildcat was clawing at the covers and bucking against my face as I teased her some more. When she came on my face, I licked up every drop and couldn't help but smile in satisfaction.

She was panting, and her eyes were closed. I placed a kiss on her belly and reached for the bedside drawer. Little did she realize, I had quite the stash of toys and I intended to use as many of them as possible before the night was over. I pulled out a smaller vibrator than the one we'd used before. I sat on my knees and pulled her closer until my cock was lined up with her slit. When the toy whirred to life, her eyes went wide.

"Just how many of those things do you have?"

I smirked. "You're going to find out, one toy at a time."

The smile she gave me made my dick jerk, and some pre-cum dribbled onto her. I rubbed it into her skin before easing the head of my cock inside of her. I'd always wanted to try this, but I'd never had a partner who inspired me as much as Josie did. I made sure she was comfortable and then placed the toy against her clit.

Josie gasped and her back arched as her hands fisted the covers.

"The only way you're getting more of my dick is if you take it," I told her.

"T-take it?"

"I want you to fuck yourself with my cock. Use me like a sex toy."

Her eyes dilated and her lips parted.

I circled her clit with the toy, and it wasn't long before her hips were pumping, and she accepted more of my dick. I switched speeds on the toy until it pulsed and buzzed against her little bud. Josie cried out and began fucking my cock. I wrapped an arm around her waist and hauled her against my body before I flipped onto my back. She straddled me; my cock buried deep inside of her. I teased and tormented her with the toy, switching from fast to slow speeds, then changing the rhythm. She was riding me fast and hard when she screamed out her release, milking every drop of cum from my cock.

Josie fell across my chest, her hair plastered to her sweat coated skin.

"So, how do you like my toy collection so far?" I asked, smiling.

"If they're all as good as that one, you may have to go buy more."

I couldn't help but laugh as I cuddled her close. Who knew when I was checking out the reverend's daughter that I'd end up with my perfect match?

Epilogue

Josie

"I swear to God, if you ever come near me again with that monster cock of yours, I'll cut off your balls and shove them down your throat," I growled as I stared at Ty with narrowed eyes. He looked both amused and terrified as his hand cupped his balls.

I bore down on his hand, probably squeezing the life out of it, but fuck if this wasn't the worst pain I'd ever felt in my entire life. I'd asked for drugs at least three times and the nurse just smiled patiently and told me there wasn't time. Fuck that! She'd better make time. I was *not* having this baby without some serious meds. It wasn't my fault I'd gone from my contractions being six minutes apart to three minutes apart within the span of an hour.

Sweat soaked the hospital gown I was wearing as the doctor checked me once more. My pussy had seen more action tonight than it had in weeks. If baby Grant didn't make his appearance soon, I was going to tell them to cut me open and pull him out. How did women do this shit? Another spike of pain hit me as a contraction gripped my stomach and wrapped around my back. I ground my teeth together to keep from screaming.

"Well, I have good news, Josie," the doctor said. "It's time to push."

Halle-freakin-lujah.

"Now, after the next contraction comes, I want you to push as hard as you can."

Not a problem. I'd push the kid out so hard they'd need a quarterback to catch him. Did quarterbacks do the catching? Fuck.

I pushed as hard as I could when the time came,

and poor Ty's fingers turned purple. He winced but didn't utter a word of complaint. I had to hand it to him; I'd been a super bitch since the contractions started and he'd taken it in stride, murmuring words of comfort to me, even when I snapped back and threatened his manhood.

"You're doing great, wildcat. Almost there." He smoothed my hair back with his free hand.

I panted between pushes and glared at him. "I hate you right now. You know that, right?"

"No, you don't. You love me, and as soon as Grant is snuggled in your arms, you'll remember that."

"One more big push," the doctor said.

I bore down so hard I forgot to breathe and was rewarded with the sweet sound of my baby boy crying. Tears filled my eyes as I watched the nurse clean him up. When she settled him in my arms, the hours of pain and discomfort faded away.

"He's perfect, isn't he?" I said in awe as I counted his fingers and toes.

"You expected any less? I mean, look at his parents. We're pretty spectacular."

I smiled at him. "I'm sorry I threatened to neuter you."

"Yeah, well, you're still not allowed near any sharp objects anytime soon."

"Do you want to hold him?" I asked.

He looked scared but held out his arms. I placed Grant in Ty's arms and watched as he cradled our son against his massive chest. I'd never seen a more touching scene and tears sprang to my eyes. Ty was demanding in the bedroom, but I'd quickly discovered that when it came to me -- and now our son -- he was a big softie. There wasn't anything he wouldn't do for us, and it made me love him even more.

"I love you, Ty. You know that, right?"

He leaned down and kissed me softly. "Love you too, wildcat. Deflowering the reverend's daughter was the best thing I ever did. It landed me you and created this handsome little devil."

I'd decided against breastfeeding, so the nurse handed Ty a bottle. I felt a twinge of envy that I did all the work, and he got the first feeding, but after I nearly broke his hand, I figured he'd earned it. As I watched father and son, my eyes slowly drifted closed, a smile on my face. I had more happiness and love in my heart than I'd ever thought possible. Who'd have guessed that the sexy, bad boy cop would turn out to be the man of my dreams?

Harley Wylde

Harley Wylde is the International Bestselling Author of the Dixie Reapers MC, Devil's Boneyard MC, and Hades Abyss MC series. When Harley's writing, her motto is the hotter the better -- off the charts sex, commanding men, and the women who can't deny them. If you want men who talk dirty, are sexy as hell, and take what they want, then you've come to the right place. She doesn't shy away from the dangers and nastiness in the world, bringing those realities to the pages of her books, but always gives her characters a happily-ever-after and makes sure the bad guys get what they deserve.

The times Harley isn't writing, she's thinking up naughty things to do to her husband, drinking copious amounts of Starbucks, and reading. She loves to read and devours a book a day, sometimes more. She's also fond of TV shows and movies from the 1980's, as well as paranormal shows from the 1990's to today, even though she'd much rather be reading or writing. You can find out more about Harley or enter her monthly giveaway on her website. Be sure to join her newsletter while you're there to learn more about discounts, signing events, and other goodies!

Harley at Changeling: changelingpress.com/harley-wylde-a-196

Changeling Press E-Books

More Sci-Fi, Fantasy, Paranormal, and BDSM adventures available in e-book format for immediate download at ChangelingPress.com -- Werewolves, Vampires, Dragons, Shapeshifters and more -- Erotic Tales from the edge of your imagination.

What are E-Books?

E-books, or electronic books, are books designed to be read in digital format -- on your desktop or laptop computer, notebook, tablet, Smart Phone, or any electronic e-book reader.

Where can I get Changeling Press E-Books?

Changeling Press e-books are available at ChangelingPress.com, Amazon, Apple Books, Barnes & Noble, and Kobo/Walmart.

Changeling Press, LLC

ChangelingPress.com